The Midwest Farmer's Guide to Love

A Demeter Society Story
BOOK 2

For Mom and Melanie Lee

Chapter One

In Which Things Get Steamy

Chloe drove down the county highway, full of the joys of early autumn. The red speckled leaves on the trees suggested a riotous celebration of nature's beauty rather than a hint of the dormant season to come, and the sun shone bright in a crisp blue sky. Her windows were open, her blonde hair whipped in the breeze, and the hood of her truck was smoking… Wait…Was that smoke? What had started out as a faintly discernible wisp soon became a solid wall, and in the short time it took for her to come to a full stop, the haze had become so thick that she couldn't see a thing in front of her.

The cloud of smoke dissipated just long enough to reveal that nothing but an uncut meadow of wispy brown grass stood between her and her destination. She supposed she might be able make it there if she kept driving. But no, she knew better. That choice could mean the end of her engine. On top of that, she'd have to confess to her mechanic, who also happened to be her father, that she had driven with a smoking hood for a quarter of a mile. She could picture him now. He wasn't much of a talker, but he had a mean head shake.

She called Bea, who would be waiting for her at the farm. There was no answer. Her goat-farming best friend was probably outside, working in the barn. Chloe leaped out of the truck, slammed the door, and yelled a bit until she felt better, kicking the gravel for emphasis. A satisfying shower of pebbles rained down on the baked and weathered road.

Turning back to her truck, she caressed it along the light blue stripe that ran along the length of its side. "Sorry I slammed your door, Old Blue. I'm not mad at you. None of this is your fault. We'll have you fixed up in no time."

"Umm...Can I help you?" There was someone behind her. Of course there was. Where had he come from? More importantly, how long had he been standing there? Long enough to observe her roadside meltdown?

She swiped her hair out of her eyes and spun around. A man stood there, right on the edge of the road where the parched grass met the gravel. He scratched his head under his cap and considered her with a bemused grin on his face. It was Arthur.

Unlike Chloe, who was becoming sweatier and more disheveled by the minute, Arthur was flawless, like he hadn't been toiling in a barn since five this morning. His navy t-shirt, which matched the body of Old Blue almost identically, was tucked into a pair of jeans, exposing a thick metal belt buckle. The shirt was snug around his arms and loose everywhere else. He had nice arms, the kinds of arms that a person got from hefting bales of hay from dawn to dusk.

Chloe shook her head, snapping out of it. Having a meltdown on the side of the road was not well paired with staring strangers in the belt buckle. She felt lightheaded and leaned over, gripping her knees. Her dizziness had nothing to do with Arthur's square jaw and the cute dimple on his left cheek. She had just been thrown off by her sticky circumstances.

"My engine is smoking," she said with as much dignity as she could muster. "The radiator must've sprung a leak."

Arthur nodded and scrutinized the truck. He didn't have to. It had become a bit less obvious with the passage of time, but it was undeniably smoking like a delinquent behind a tree.

"I can see that." He still stood there with his head tilted, grinning at her.

Chloe was tempted to tell him that the show was over and he could move along, but she was working on her manners this week. Besides, she had lost her standing to claim the moral high ground when it came to gawking.

Instead, she considered her options. It was unseasonably hot by the side of the road. Even in Wisconsin, her fair skin could look forward to a red and blistered fate if she waited out in the open too long for her engine to cool. She wished she would've worn her gardening hat.

Arthur might be able to help, though. The covered porch in front of his neat white farmhouse looked cool and inviting. It housed a bevy of potted plants and wicker furniture. There was even a swing hanging from the ceiling on one side. An American flag stuck out next to the steps, rippling in the breeze. She had always wanted a covered porch like that. Sitting on one would be some consolation for the way this day had begun. If he was like most farmers, he probably wouldn't be stingy with the lemonade either.

"Do you mind if I wait at your house for a bit until I can get my truck going again?" she asked. "I'm on my way to Cedar Hollow Farm. I would hoof it over there, but I have a bed full of tools."

Arthur raised his politely dubious eyebrows, sauntered over to her truck, and leaned over the edge of the bed, peering into the back. He would have seen that there were, indeed, far more tools back there than they could both carry together.

"You're not kidding. Well, come along," he said, heading back to the farmhouse. Trotting behind him, Chloe went up the steps and made a beeline for the swing. Arthur went inside then, giving her a chance to regroup.

She leaned back and pushed her feet off the ground, starting her seat swinging. Having driven by this house countless times, she thought she had some idea of what it was like, but she'd never seen it up close before. It struck her as being very spruce and winsome for the lodgings of a bachelor farmer. The porch floor had been recently stained with a sealant that looked like whitewash. It bore signs of having been recently swept, and a pot of yellow chrysanthemums sat beside the welcome mat. There was even a little cement turtle perched near her feet.

Was the rest of the farm this picturesque? She hadn't been paying attention when she followed behind Arthur, because she was distracted by...well, what he lacked in conversational skills he made up for with other, more visually-based charms.

She stood up and peeked around the edge of the house. Holsteins grazed in front of a classic red barn. A barn quilt was tucked under its gabled eves and featured the silhouette of a cat looking out a window. The chicken coop appeared to be decorated by children's hands. Its colorful painted flowers were punctuated by little round bees and ladybugs.

Chloe slid back into the swing, and Arthur returned in a moment with lemonade. Joy! She knew he would come through. Ice clinked in a tall glass cup decorated with strawberries. This guy was full of surprises.

He seemed to have gone to her father's finishing school for eloquent men, though. He handed her the glass, said, "Whelp, better get to it," tipped his battered baseball cap to her, and walked around the house.

She took a sip of the lemonade. It was delicious. It tasted fresh squeezed, and was that...lavender syrup? She closed her eyes. The late September day was quiet. Aside from the occasional car passing by, the only sounds came from the cows in the field and a tractor rumbling in the distance. The stillness was interrupted by a high-pitched squeak coming towards her from the direction of the barn. Arthur ambled back with a massive wheelbarrow.

"You're going to trash your truck if you drive it like that," he said.

He walked over to the truck bed, lifted out the tools, and deposited them in the wheelbarrow. Chloe set her lemonade on the ground, jumped up, and sprinted across the road. "Careful with those, they're my life's work. Here, let me help you."

She plucked a pitchfork out of his hand and set it in the wheelbarrow like she was lying a baby down to sleep. He nodded and continued to transfer the tools, using even more care this time. That grin was still plastered on his face, like he couldn't have found her more amusing. It was irritating. She didn't see what was so funny. She'd just had some car trouble, that's all. And these tools were really important to her. If it wasn't for them, she'd still be a cog in a factory. Instead, she got to empower other women to pick up their pitchforks and make things grow.

"You're intimidated by my tools," she said.

"Pardon?"

"They're built especially for women. I get it. A lot of men are taken aback by my business."

"I didn't realize..."

"If I had a penny for every time a guy asked me why I didn't make tools especially for men too, I would be able to buy a big sign that said "Because all the other tools are already designed for men.""

"Catchy."

"It wouldn't have to say *exactly* that." That was

the essence of the thing though. A sign wouldn't cost her much to make at all. She'd think of a better slogan. It would save her a lot of grief.

He raised his eyebrows and nodded. "Huh."

As cavernous as the wheelbarrow was, it could only accommodate about a third of her supplies.

"Sorry," said Arthur, "It didn't look like you had that much stuff. We could fit everything in my truck."

"That's alright. Now that we've got everything loaded up, I'd hate to have to move it again. When we get to the farm, I'll ask Bea if she can come back with her van."

Arthur trundled off down the road. Chloe walked along beside him, trying to match him stride for stride, and waited for him to say something. He had hardly spoken two words to her since she'd been marooned in front of his house, and she didn't want to keep babbling.

She distracted herself by hopping into the ditch and plucking a clump of goldenrod. When she accidentally pulled it up by the roots, an abundance of dirt cascaded onto her shoes and legs. She knocked the soil off as well as she could and ran to catch up to Arthur, who hadn't noticed that she had fallen behind. The flower stems proved to be too stringy for her to break, and she threw them into the ditch behind his back.

Out of distractions, Chloe filled the silence with more chatter.

"It's been fantastic to have your mom in our farm group. Sarah's a wise woman. The other day she said to me, 'It's lovely that you're so confident dear, but please remember that some things are better left unsaid. Once a bird has left your hand, you can never get it back.' It was the best advice I'd been given in a long time. I have a tendency to blurt out whatever comes to mind. So this week, I'm working on screening myself a bit. Not too much, just a bit. There's no need to go overboard." She laughed.

"Yup," he said. "That's my mom for ya." She must have given him the same advice about thinking before he spoke. He really took it to heart.

"It's been really hot this month. The nights are getting cooler though. I just love September. It's my favorite."

He grunted.

Maybe that meant that he loved September too, or perhaps it meant that he hated it. The possibilities were endless. How exciting. Chloe giggled silently to herself, and a chuckle popped out before she could stop it. Arthur glanced over at her. Chloe decided right then and there to stop trying to engage him. At this rate, he was going to think that she was a lunatic, and they weren't even halfway there.

Silence seemed to suit Arthur splendidly. As they bumped along the road, the tools banged together with a clank and a crunch despite his caution, causing Chloe to wince.

"I can take over for while," she offered.

"I've got it," he said. They couldn't get to Cedar Hollow Farm soon enough.

Chapter Two

In Which Chloe Breaks Her Oath to Tone it Down

Bea was in the barn with the goats, the straw, and a lovely looking pitchfork of superb design. When she finally registered their presence, she gazed at them blankly, as if it was taking a moment for her to process the unexpected pair.

"Oh," she said, continuing to jab into the straw and spread it around. "Sorry guys, I didn't see you there."

"No worries," Chloe said. "We've only been waiting fifteen minutes."

"What?"

"I'm kidding. We just got here."

"Oh good. You scared me. I get into something out here and everything else fades away."

"You should see me when I'm in my garage," Chloe said. "My sister Betsy came by while I was working one day and asked if she could borrow my bike for the weekend. I said yes, and the next day I was calling to warn her that there was a bike thief in the neighborhood."

"I remember that. You called me too," said Bea.

"Oh. That's actually kind of embarrassing."

"No way. You've got focus."

Arthur gently set down the wheelbarrow. "I gotta run. Let me know if you need any more help," he said, addressing them both. He strode away without looking back.

When he was out of earshot, Chloe said, "Well, he's a man of few words."

Bea dusted her hands off on her jeans and joined her at the barn door. "He's always been the quiet one in the Watson family. But what happened? Where's your truck?"

"It overheated right in front of chatty-magee's house. I was going to wait and let it cool down for a bit, but there had been enough smoke that I decided it would be better not to try to drive it." She didn't mention that it was a certain reticent yet handsome farmer who had actually made the suggestion.

"Good call," Bea said. She eyed up the jumble of tools. "Is this everything, or are there more in the truck?"

"There are a lot more. This isn't even half."

"You've been busy lately."

"What can I say? I'm a woman of action."

"I'd say. We're going to run out of garages trying to keep up with you."

"I know. I felt really awkward about asking you do this."

"I could tell. I was afraid you were mustering up the courage to ask me for a kidney or something, instead of just some garage space. I know you don't like to depend on anyone, but that's what your friends are here for. Besides, you're always the first person to volunteer when we need help. I'm excited you're letting me help you for a change."

"Well be careful what you wish for, because I have big dreams."

"Go for them. I'm serious. We'll figure it out. For now though, I should be able to squeeze the rest of your tools into my van. Let's go."

They headed over to the delivery van, which was parked on the far side of the farmhouse, and Bea dragged open the sliding door. She pulled out an old rocking chair.

"I found this on the side of the road, and I couldn't pass it up."

It was missing a seat, but it looked solid, like it was made of quality wood. Bea stashed it behind a fluffy red burning bush next to the house.

"I'm going to fix it up for my mom. I'll secret it away later." She closed the door, and Chloe admired the curvy lettering that formed the words Cedar Hollow Farm.

"Your nephew painted that script on your van, right?" Chloe asked.

"He did. He's pretty artsy."

"I'd say. It looks professional. Do you think he'd do a project for me?"

"I'm sure he'd be thrilled. You're not thinking of painting Old Blue, are you?"

"No. I need a sign for trade shows, something like: *Bare Roots Tools: They're Designed For Women, Get*

Over It."

"That's perfect."

"Not too punchy?"

"If anything, it's not punchy enough."

"Ooh. You're right. I think I'll add *Bub* at the end."

Bea laughed.

"I'm serious," said Chloe. "He's hired."

"I'll let him know. I get the feeling he'll get a kick out of this commission."

They climbed into the van and Bea backed into the road, heading towards the truck. "I should've seen this coming. Old Blue is thirty years old, and she's never had a major issue. It had to happen some time."

"Same age as us," Bea replied. "I haven't had any major issues either, but I'm starting to see a couple of grays."

"Oh please, you're just like Old Blue: in pristine condition. The grays add character."

Chloe's beloved truck was visible now. It looked forlorn there, all alone on the gravel shoulder. She knew it was a bit silly, but she really was attached to the old pickup, which had been purchased used from a retired farmer. There wasn't a spot of rust on her, then or now. Initially, she'd been just plain Blue. She had recently earned the additional moniker Old, as they'd been together for almost a decade.

Bea passed the truck, did a u-turn, and pulled up behind it. As they went by Arthur's house, Chloe couldn't help noticing that he was outside, carrying a pail from his garage to the barn. He waved at them without looking over and carried on.

"What's the deal with Arthur?" asked Chloe. She was still irked by the way he had quietly chuckled at her. She found a Fleet Farm receipt on the seat next to her and started to fold it, accordion style. Oops, Bea might need that. She smoothed it back out and set it down.

"The deal? What do you mean?" Bea had been ready to get out of the van. She slid her hand off the handle and turned to face her friend. Chloe noticed a sly grin on Bea's face and hoped she wasn't think-ing that her interest in the farmer that was anything other than basic curiosity. He was just an interesting person, in a way that kind of got on her nerves.

"I mean, what's he like?" Chloe asked. "He's been your neighbor for years now. He's lived here basically all his life. But none of us know him very well. Or is it just me?"

"No. It's not just you. I think he's really quiet with everyone, like you said. I've only talked to him a handful of times since he moved in a few years ago, when he's stopped by to help us with one thing or another. Remember his twin brother George though? He was so popular. I think Arthur took the role of the quiet guy who was into his farming and hunting and things like that."

"That makes sense. Everyone carves out his own niche. And yes, I remember George. How could I forget?" He was as handsome as Arthur, with the added bonus of being athletic and personable.

"Didn't you two date for a while?" Bea asked.

"No, that opportunity passed me by I'm afraid, but I'm pretty sure he 'dated' half the women in town before he left. That's probably why he never made a repeat appearance. He'd exhausted his prospects."

"Huh. He really hasn't been back, has he? I'd never noticed, but now that you mention it, I don't think I've seen him at all since he left for college. That's odd. His whole family's here. He must come back for holidays."

"Or maybe he's an international spy," said Chloe, "and he comes back in disguise."

"Probably so." Perspiration was beading on Bea's forehead. It was getting really hot in here, time to get a move on.

They hopped out and transferred the shovels and pitchforks from the truck to the van. Chloe was gratified to see that her friend also took great care with them, piling them neatly like the pieces of crafts-woman-ship that they were. It didn't take long to load them all, and they were soon on their way back. Calling her dad, Chloe reported what had happened.

"Yup," he said, "she'll need some work." He hung up.

"Is he coming?" Bea asked.

"I'm going to assume that someone will be here eventually."

Now that she had called him, Chloe was becoming anxious. She hoped that Old Blue would be ok. She definitely couldn't afford a new truck right now, and she was really attached to the one she had. The costs and uncertainty of starting Bare Roots Tools had sneaked up on her. She knew it would be worth it in the end, but she'd experienced more than a few sleepless nights since quitting her salaried day job.

She was about to confide her concerns to her friend, who could certainly relate, having recently started her own goat cheese operation, but the expression on Bea's face suggested that she was somewhere else entirely.

"Thinking about Wes?" Chloe asked.

"Yes, how did you know?"

"Really? You're too funny. Your 'thinking about Wes' look is becoming iconic."

"Well I'm glad to hear I'm so transparent. I'm pretty sure everyone in town knew I was smitten with him before I did." Bea took a wide turn into the driveway that led up to the barn and parked.

"Yeah. Everybody knew."

Bea laughed. "To answer your question, yes, I was thinking about him. We're taking a final swim in the pond tonight. It can't stay this hot forever, so we're enjoying it while we can."

"He's willing to get in the water now? That's progress. Wasn't he convinced that there was a devious snapping turtle lying in wait for him?" Chloe hopped out and slid open the side door. She was pleased to see that her tools looked unscathed after their big adventure.

"Apparently he's decided that the turtle is good luck now," Bea said, pulling open the door on the driver's side.

The two women unloaded the tools behind the house near the vegetable garden. A scarecrow, suspended from a wooden post, supervised the operation. His flannel shirt and canvas pants, cast-offs from Bea's dad or brother, had faded to gray over the course of the summer. His burlap face featured a lopsided grin shadowed by a floppy brimmed hat. The goats crowded around the fence to observe the proceedings as well.

"Remember how we used to sneak over to that pond as kids and swim all the time?" Chloe asked, picking up a trio of shovels.

"How could I forget? We all thought we were getting away with something, but I have no doubt that our parents knew what we were up to."

"Oh, for sure. No one would ever let their kids do that now, though. 'A murky pond with no supervision and a rusty metal bridge to jump off of? What could go wrong? Sure kids, go ahead.'" She laughed. "Those were the days. Where should we store these?" She set the shovels in the grass.

"There's a spot cleared out in the garage. Let's empty this wheelbarrow first. Then we can fill it up with what's left."

They trundled back and forth with their precious cargo. When all the tools were tidied away, the empty wheelbarrow remained. "I can run this back over to Arthur," Chloe said, grabbing the handles and swiveling it towards the road. "I know you have a lot to do around here."

"That would be fantastic, if you don't mind."

Chloe marched back down the road towards Arthur's farm. She balanced the wheelbarrow with one hand as she peeled her sweaty shirt away from her chest to let in a breeze. A horsefly buzzed around her head, and she swatted it away. Her shirt and shorts were lined with stripes of dirt.

When she got to Arthur's driveway, there was no sign of him, but she thought she heard someone in the barn. When she got there, however, there was no one to be seen. No farmers, anyway. A few sleek black and white cows stood in their stalls, munching on straw. No matter how often she saw them from a distance, the mass of them up close startled her. She reached out to stroke the velvety nose of the closest one, but it shied away.

She turned around. Maybe she should leave before she could disrupt the peace any further. Everything in the barn was as immaculate and orderly as the covered porch. The only thing out of place was a sprinkling of sawdust beneath a workbench near the entrance, evidence of a recent project. Tools hung on pegs along the wall. It even smelled good in the barn, sweet and dry. A piglet scooted past Chloe's ankles and she leaped in surprise. It hopped away, out the open door, making tiny squealing noises as it ran.

"Hello?" she called. No answer. Where could he be?

She went back outside. Arthur was coming out of the chicken coop with a wire basket full of brown eggs. Again with that amused grin.

"Hey," she said. "I was just dropping off your wheelbarrow. Thanks for letting me use it."

"Yup," he replied. "Any time."

"Well, see you." She should walk away and not say another word, and she knew it. Once the bird was out, she couldn't get it back and all that. But then again... "I was talking to my truck before. I could tell you thought it was amusing, that I was amusing, but I'm attached to her. To it. I'm attached to it." Wow. She was a conversational athlete around this guy.

"Yup." He headed for his house with the eggs. Did that mean he *did* think it was funny or that he understood her fondness for her truck?

"I talk to my tractor too," he called over his shoulder. He disappeared through his side door. It slapped shut with a bang.

Chloe hadn't been able to see his expression. Was he making fun of her? The infuriating part was, she wouldn't care if he wasn't so darned good-looking. It made her feel shallow, and that annoyed her even more.

"Bye," she yelled as she strode away. She knew he couldn't hear her from inside the house, but it made her feel better to yell again. Good riddance, she wanted to add, but didn't.

When she got back to Cedar Hollow, the safe farm with no discombobulating farm boys lurking in it, Bea offered to drive her to her dad's garage. The offer was eagerly accepted. Delivering her tools had taken a bit longer than Chloe had anticipated, but she wasn't sorry about it. She had gotten to spend a little extra time with her best friend today. She loved hearing about her and Wes. They had reconnected after over a decade apart, and Chloe enjoyed basking in their glow every now and then. She certainly didn't have anyone to glow about at the moment.

In truth, Chloe had never found anyone that could hold her interest long enough for her to care about them like that. And, as long as she was being honest, no one had ever been all that attached to her either. There had been that guy at work a couple of years back. He'd been good for a laugh, but he wasn't serious about anything, including her. When he moved, they had tried to make the long distance thing work, but it fizzled out as quickly as it had begun. There was that chef too. He wasn't all bad; he had been part of the reason that she had gotten into gardening, after all. But beyond that, their relationship had been a disaster. She preferred not to think about him.

Now that she was working from home, her dating pool had shrunk even further. There weren't very many single men to choose from around Namur. There were lots of old Belgian farmers and some younger ones, but most of the men her age were already spoken for. Apparently the men that were available found her entertaining. Oh well. She'd much rather be entertaining than boring.

If only she could've known just how entertaining things were about to get, Chloe may have reconsidered her priorities.

Chapter Three

In Which an Attempt is Made to Rally the Troops

Bea dropped Chloe off in front of her dad's shop. The low gray building was one of many on Main Street and it wasn't much to look at, consisting of nothing but an office and three garage stalls, but it was as much an iconic part of downtown as the old library and the town hall.

Chloe peeked in the window next to the entrance. A neon sign announced that they were open, but the front counter was unmanned. She walked in anyway, passing through the office and heading into the garage to see if they had started on Old Blue yet. Sure enough, her dad had the truck on a lift. He and Karl, the only other mechanic, were working on her already.

The shop was suffused with the smell of grease, motor oil, and rubber tires that also permeated her dad's clothes and hair. For others it was chocolate chip cookies or a baking pie, but for Chloe the smell of car parts reminded her of home. Surveying the bulletin board, she pulled down a poster advertising the Kermiss harvest festival, which had already taken place, and flipped her dad's antique tractors calendar from August to September. She should stop in more often to check up on him. He was a great mechanic, but he had a one track mind.

"How is she, Dad?" she asked.

"Cripes!" Her dad came out from beneath the truck and sat up, running his hand over his newly shaven head and pushing his glasses farther up on his nose. He was still getting used to wearing them.

"You startled me," he said. "I didn't know you were here. She's looking ok. A hose to the radiator came loose. We need to replace it. It won't take long, and she'll be right as rain." He was a little more open to chatting when it came to talking shop. "Good thing you didn't drive it like this. You wouldn't believe the things that people try to do with their trucks these days."

"I know, right? People are crazy." *Yikes. That had been close.*

He was about to go back to work, pulling a wrench out of the pocket of his coveralls, when a bell dinged at the service counter. He did an about-face, leaving to greet a customer.

Greet was probably too strong a word, Chloe thought. But he would be listening and responding adequately. People must not mind his fortress-like demeanor. The shop was always hopping, probably because he was so skilled and honest.

Karl popped out from under Old Blue. "Hey, while he's gone, did you hear the latest about your sister?" he asked. He spoke quietly and swiftly, as if he didn't want his boss to overhear. The wrinkles next to his eyes deepened, and he stroked his beard. Neither were promising signs.

"Oh no. Is this new? I haven't heard anything this week. Do I even want to know?"

"I don't want to tell you, but I think you might be able to help."

She felt a headache starting already. What had Betsy done now? Chloe was still recovering from the notorious water tower debacle. She sat down in a folding chair along the wall and got ready for whatever was coming.

"I was at the tavern last night playing darts with a bunch of guys," Karl said, "when we heard a ruckus over by the pool table. It was Betsy. She had been way over-served and was dancing on it with one of her friends."

"On a Wednesday night?"

"I thought the same thing. It was really weird. I mean, it was the middle of the week. The bar was full of a bunch of the regulars sitting around, and then there they were, whooping it up."

"Ed couldn't have been thrilled about that."

"He sure wasn't. You know how he is about the surface of that table. He told them to get down; they refused, acted like they didn't hear him. So he lifted them off and told them to make themselves scarce for the rest of the night."

Ok, this wasn't as awful as Chloe had feared. Yes, it was cringe worthy, but it wasn't like Betsy had hurt anyone. Maybe it would serve as a lesson for her. She wouldn't show her face there again for a long time.

As it turned out, the story wasn't over.

"Betsy got really mad," said Karl. "I think she was embarrassed. I was embarrassed for her anyway. She still had the drink in her hand. She acted like she was going to walk away, but then she turned around and threw it in Ed's face. He told her she was banned from the bar and called them a cab."

There it was. That was actually really terrible. Betsy was sure to be hiding out right now until this passed, but she couldn't lie low forever. She had to go in to work, and she waitressed at Emma's Café of all places. Tongues were surely already wagging there.

"I've heard she's been at the taverns more often lately," he said. "Normally I wouldn't care, but if she's doing things like that...I just thought she might be having other issues."

"Agreed, but I'm not sure exactly what's going on. She doesn't talk to me about that kind of stuff. Did you say anything to my dad about it?"

"Nah. We don't talk much either. But I wanted to tell you. Betsy and I used to be close. I'm not sure what's going on with her, but maybe you could do something to reach out. She seems like she's adrift right now, but I don't think she's too far gone." Karl looked unsure if he should've said anything.

"I'm glad you told me. You're a philosopher mechanic, did you know that?" asked Chloe.

"I do what I can."

"See, this is why you've withstood the test of

time here."

"What do you mean?"

"You ponder things but you're not too chatty. The last guy who had your job was fired after three months."

"I heard about that. I assumed he wasn't any good."

"Yeah. That's what my dad claimed, but he seemed fine to me. I suspect it was really because he asked his boss to go ice fishing one too many times."

"What?"

"I know. It doesn't make sense. It drove my dad crazy though. He already has one friend that he doesn't talk to. He's not interested in having any more."

"Wow. Thanks for the heads up. I feel like I dodged a bullet."

"What do you mean?"

"I was going to ask if he wanted to come up to our deer camp this year."

"You're going to want to scratch that plan if you value your position."

"Noted."

"Back to Betsy, the problem with her is..." She stopped. Her dad had just marched back in. He ducked back under the truck. Karl joined him with an innocent expression on his face. They rattled around, pausing to grab various tools while Chloe paced back and forth.

She appreciated the quiet, because she needed to sort through her thoughts. What had she been about to say? The problem with Betsy is...what? She didn't know exactly, but she was determined to find out.

What would her dad say about this? Ed was sure to tell him eventually. Or would he? No. It was too awkward a subject for those two to broach. As long as Betsy didn't keep causing issues, Ed would probably let it go.

Chloe had tried to talk to her dad about Betsy before, when she wasn't half as bad as she was now, but he wasn't interested in intervening. That was somewhat understandable. She was an adult after all, and for the most part she kept things together.

Betsy had her own little house in Chloe's neighborhood. They often hosted each other for dinner. If they didn't talk about anything too serious, and Betsy wasn't interested in that anyway, they had a fun time together. She hadn't ever gotten into any serious trouble. Even this, as out of line as it was, wouldn't be the end of the world.

To the extent that she did some questionable things though, Betsy's trajectory wasn't predictable. Their dad wasn't wild at all, obviously. Apparently their mom was as a teenager, but she had her kids young and settled down before she could get into too much mischief.

Maybe that was part of the problem though. She egged Betsy on, living vicariously through her exploits. She thought Betsy's boyfriends were charming and hilarious. To be honest, some of them were, but they weren't the kinds of guys that you wanted dating your sister.

Chloe was struck with sudden inspiration. Maybe if her mom knew how bad things had gotten, she would finally try to intervene. Her sense of humor wouldn't extend to a friend of theirs getting a drink tossed in his face. Why was it always up to Chloe to sort these things out? Her mom's salon was just a short jaunt down the road. She could walk over there, talk to her, and try to exert some real influence on this family for a change.

"Hey Dad," she said.

"Yeah?"

"I'm going over to the salon to talk to Mom for a bit. I'll be back in a while."

Chloe stepped onto the sidewalk along Main Street. School had just let out for the day and a bus blew by, full of bouncing kids on their way back home. A boy stuck his tongue out at her and she did it right back. She waved at the barber through the window and turned to go into her mom's shop. Tammi's Cut N Curl was written in big swirly pink letters on the glass door.

Her mom stood at the counter, her nails clicking as she typed at a computer. Her bleach blonde hair was swept back into an updo, and she wore a pink paisley apron over a form fitting dress. At the ping of the bell over the door, she looked up and flung her hands over her heart.

"I can't believe it. My middle daughter is finally getting a haircut."

Chloe had twisted her hair into a single long

braid after the truck incident. She swept it behind her now, as if protecting it from her mother's scissors.

"I'm not here for a haircut, Mom. I want to talk to you about Betsy."

"Oh boy. Listen, if you really want to go there, I'll make you a deal. You let me cut your hair, and I'll let you tell me all about Betsy." Her mom rolled her eyes. Chloe couldn't believe that she hadn't outgrown that yet.

Chloe turned as if ready to leave, and her mom continued. "You haven't had your hair cut in almost a year. I know, because if you're not letting me cut it, you're certainly not paying anyone else to do it."

Chloe was ready to protest, but it was true, she couldn't remember the last time she'd gotten a haircut. She was busy though. Who had that kind of time?

"Your sister's wedding is coming up and you have split ends. You don't want to have split ends for a wedding," her mom said, widening her eyes. Chloe really didn't care about her split ends and she doubted that anyone else did either, but she knew that her mom wasn't bluffing. If she wanted to be heard out, getting a haircut was the price she would have to pay.

"Okay, you've got me," said Chloe, plopping into a chair.

Her mom hurried over as if worried that her daughter would escape if she didn't act fast. She slipped Chloe's grubby hair tie off the end of her plait and, pinching it between her thumb and forefinger, threw it in the garbage. Once she had untangled the braid, she brushed through clumps of matted hair while Chloe tilted her head away and scrunched her face.

"What happened here? Your hair's all tangled and smoky," her mom said, wrinkling her nose.

"I was driving with the window open when my car started smoking. Dad's working on it right now. It'll be fine."

"I don't know. If you ask me, this is one big mess you have going on back here."

"Not my hair Mom, my truck. Old Blue will be fine."

"Oh goodie." Was that sarcasm? She never had approved of the truck.

"You've got me where you want me. Can I talk to you about Betsy now?"

"Just a minute. You need to tell me how you want your hair cut first. Do you have a style in mind?" She snapped out of auto-pilot and regarded Chloe's hair again. "Forget I asked. I'm just cutting it. I know you don't care but I do, so I'm going to make it pretty."

"That's fine. Please don't cut it too short though, I need to be able to pull it up when I'm working."

"Hmm," her mom said noncommittally and got to work.

"Back to Betsy, she was dancing on the pool table at Ed's Tavern..."

"How fun."

How did it fall to Chloe to explain this? "No mom. It's not fun."

"Oh please, you used to be a riot yourself. Are you jealous because you have to be a serious businesswoman now? I get it. I really do. There are a lot of pressures that come along with owning your own business." She popped her gum. "But we need to remember that other people don't need to be so solemn all the time."

Was she lumping herself in with the solemn people? She had penciled on her eyebrows in an arch so high that they made her look permanently surprised. She wore two inch heels to stand up cutting hair all day. There was nothing solemn about her.

"Yes, mom, I agree that it's great to be spontaneous, but maybe not in the local tavern on a Wednesday night." Her objection received no response. "I haven't gotten to the concerning part, though. She threw a drink in Ed's face when he asked her to leave. She's gotten herself banned from the tavern."

Her mom stopped spritzing her hair. Apparently Betsy had gone too far even for her.

"Ok, I'll have a talk with her. You're right. That's completely out of line. If she wants to let her hair down, she should consider taking a road trip to the city or something."

"That's not...ugh...That's not the point I'm trying to make here. It's time for her to mellow out a bit. This is getting concerning."

"Like I said, I'll talk to her. I promise."

Her mom grabbed a scissors and started snipping. Chloe could tell by the look in her eyes that she had already moved on to considering the hairstyle that would best suit her heart shaped face.

Her mom continued to cut and trim as Chloe became increasingly alarmed by the sea of blonde strands building up around her on the linoleum floor. It had all been for naught, too. What a waste. Soon, she was spun around to face the mirror.

"What to do you think?" her beautician asked. Chloe appraised the new look. Huh. She liked it. A lot of the length had been preserved and some long layers gave more shape to her usually uniform sheet of hair.

"It's really pretty, thanks."

"What can I say? I'm a pro." She wagged her finger. Her nails were decorated with leopard print paint. "If you want to maintain it, you should come in more often. I recommend every two months. You shouldn't let it go any longer than that." She caught Chloe looking at her fancy nails and swooped in to grab her hand. "Your nails are atrocious. Look at that dirt."

Chloe pulled away and slid off the chair, removing her crinkly apron. "I was delivering tools today. They don't always look like this." They did usually look like that, and they both knew it. "I have to run, though. We'll work on my nails next time." Another statement they both knew wasn't true. "I'm going to head back over to Dad's and see if my truck is ready."

Her mom swept around the chair and brushed off the seat. "Sounds good, honey. Come back any time. I mean it."

"We'll see. You did a really nice job."

Chloe walked out the door. Well, that hadn't

been the coup she was hoping for. She could keep trying, but she'd end up with plucked brows, painted nails, and highlights. She shuddered at the thought and pulled a fresh elastic out of her pocket. She rebraided her hair and let it flop down her back.

Her truck waited for her in the parking lot. Chloe gave her a pat on the stripe. "Looking good, Old Blue. Now we can hit the road again."

Heading into the office, she found Karl waiting for her. Her dad was in the garage tinkering with an old muscle car. "Thanks for getting my truck up and running again," she said, "and for telling me about Betsy."

"Hey, no problem," he said, handing her the key. "Let me know how it goes, ok?"

"For sure." She paused in the doorway and turned around. "You know what? I'm going to go to Emma's and see if she's there. I don't want to wait. I can act like I just happened to stop in for dinner. Maybe we can talk on her break, and I'll casually bring up Ed's."

"Good luck. You probably know this, but I don't think she likes being given advice."

"You're absolutely right, but I can't claim to be innocent of harboring that family trait. I'll tread carefully."

Karl wiped his forehead with a rag and went back into the garage.

"Let's go Old Blue," Chloe said as she hopped into her truck. "We have a sister to set straight."

Chapter Four

In Which Chloe's Patience is Tested

Emma's was packed with early diners, dashing any hopes Chloe had of having a heart to heart with her sister. The two waitresses, Betsy and Emma, hurried from the kitchen to the tables with trays full of heaping dinner plates. Chloe pulled up a chair and eventually caught Betsy's eye.

"I'd love to talk right now, but it's really busy tonight," Betsy said when she finally made it to Chloe's table.

It was true. Families squished into plush red booths by the bay window that faced the road; couples sat two by two at the cafe tables. Now that she was here, Chloe noticed the gurgling of her stomach. When was the last time she ate? She eyed up the meatloaf and potatoes in front of the man at the table next to her.

"Do you want to order something?" asked Betsy, tapping her foot.

"Yes, I'll do that. I'd like what he's having." She pointed to the meatloaf. It was perfection, topped with ketchup and studded with onions.

"Coming right up."

Betsy whizzed off to take another order. Chloe had to hand it to her; she had become almost as speedy as Emma. She ran to the kitchen to yell the orders to Ernie and was back in an instant with a glass of water and some silverware before hurrying on her way again.

If they couldn't have their chat here, maybe Betsy would be willing to come over to Chloe's house that evening. She wouldn't agree to it if she knew that her older sister wanted to discuss what happened last night, though. How could she approach this? She'd have some time to think of a brilliant idea while she ate.

She didn't have long to wait. Betsy was back minutes later, presenting her with an oversized plate of meatloaf, mashed potatoes, and buttery green beans. "Enjoy," she said and zipped away.

Betsy hadn't seemed embarrassed to be out in public, but it was still early days. News didn't spread quite that fast. Who was Chloe kidding? News spread at nearly the speed of sound around here.

She scanned the room again. Did she recognize anyone? Yes. Sarah and Roy were in their usual booth. Roy was following his own principles of talking, loudly and often. Sarah must not have shared the same wisdom with him that she had imparted to Chloe and Arthur.

Chloe finished off her meatloaf and walked over to their table. When Sarah saw her, she beamed and moved over.

"This is a surprise," said Sarah. "We usually

don't see you here in the evening."

Everyone seemed to think she had turned into some kind of a reverse vampire. She did emerge in the evening sometimes. Chloe explained about her troubles with the truck and her visit to her dad's shop. "Oh dear," her friend said. "Well, I'm just happy to see that you're alright."

Roy must have sensed that he was losing his audience and jumped in with some news. "Hey, did you hear our Georgie's coming back?" He took a big bite of his sandwich.

She hadn't heard. It was funny, she hadn't thought of him in ages and now here he was, coming up twice in one day.

"Yup," said Roy, his mouth full of pastrami on rye. "He's coming back for a couple of months starting with your sister's wedding."

Oh, that's right. She had forgotten that the whole Watson family would be attending. Hannah counted their youngest daughter amongst her closest childhood friends.

Roy leaned back and patted his stomach. Chloe wondered if he wore the same denim overalls every day or if he had a closet full of them. They always looked clean and so crisp they had to have been ironed, by Sarah of course.

"Yup, George is an important businessman in the Twin Cities," he said. "He's made quite a name for himself developing real estate. He's thinking about building something on the site where the old library is now."

"Might that be considered a conflict of inter-est?" Chloe asked. Oops, not thinking before she spoke again. Self-improvement wasn't for the faint of heart.

"How so?" He paused his sandwich in mid-jour-ney on its return to his mouth.

Well, he did ask. "You're the president of the town board, right?"

"I sure am."

"And you led the charge to demolish the library, opening up the space for private business."

"I did. But..." He returned to his boasting, as if her concern had never sullied his ears. "Like I said, George is a big success. He's a chip off the old block, that one." Roy said it in a way that made Chloe won-der if he was contrasting him with his quiet twin brother Arthur.

She could tell from the look on his face that Roy was warming up to brag a bit more about his son, so she headed him off. "Speaking of George, I saw Arthur today. He helped me out when my truck broke down in front of his farm."

"How nice dear. Arthur is such a sweet boy," said Sarah.

"He was a huge help. He let me wait on his porch and hauled some of my tools over to Bea's in his wheelbarrow."

"He's handy," said Roy. "George, on the other hand, was never inclined to work with his hands. He's the kind of guy who likes to work with his mind." He tapped his temple to illustrate where George did his great thinking.

"It takes all kinds I guess," said Chloe. As much as she had been irritated by the way silent Arthur had found her so amusing, she was sorry to hear how much Roy clearly favored his twin brother.

"I better run. I'll see you tomorrow for the workshop," Chloe said to Sarah. She slid out of the booth and was turning to walk away when Roy took a parting shot.

He slapped his denim knee. "You ladies and your little club. Always looking for an excuse to get together and gab, eh?"

Chloe turned back to face him. "Yes Roy. We little ladies are looking forward to gabbing about ways to support each other in our entrepreneurial endeavors. We don't need anyone else to pave the way for us." She trusted that he understood her meaning. "Gotta love an independent woman, right?"

She smiled and looked him in the eye, daring him to say anything more. She almost did her Rosie the Riveter move but reconsidered. It would keep for another day.

Sarah diffused the situation. "Didn't you want to order dessert, dear?" she asked her husband. "We'll see you tomorrow, Chloe."

Sarah shot her a look. Chloe knew what the look meant. She had seen it many times before. It was admonishing her to be more Midwest-nice.

Chloe relaxed her fake smile and grinned. "See you," she said. Roy wasn't worth it, but why did he have to be so provoking?

And speaking of provoking, where was Betsy? Chloe scanned the room. She was still running around, and Chloe had to wait until she was behind the counter pouring coffee before she could get her attention. "Do you want to come over tonight?" Chloe asked her.

"Sure, but I'm working late." Betsy was distracted by her task and hadn't fully registered the question. It didn't take long though, before understanding started to dawn. It was no coincidence that Betsy had just made a scene last night and now Chloe was inviting her over for some sisterly bonding time.

She jumped in to explain further, before Betsy could change her mind. "I'm just in the mood to visit. Maybe we could make a salad or something, pick some veggies from my garden."

"A salad? That's all you've got? I know why you want me to come over, and I get it, ok? I know I messed up. Grace and I were just having some fun and got a little carried away."

"A little carried away?" Chloe raised her voice and a couple of the men at the counter tipped up their caps and looked at her with concern. She spoke more quietly then, taking a seat on a stool. "A little carried away? I would call that a lot carried away, personally. I don't even want to know what you would consider fully carried away."

Betsy wiped the counter with a swoosh. She accidentally swiped a salt shaker over, spilling its contents. Her wavy blonde hair was damp around her neck; she may not have been as cool and collected as she would've liked her sister to believe.

"I have to run," she said, "but I'll come over and listen to what you have to say about me and the things that I do."

There it was, the family eye roll. Chloe could take it. She didn't care. She just needed to talk a little sense into her sister. She wasn't sure if she was doing it for Betsy's sake or her own. Both of their reputations were being impacted. In all honesty, it was probably a good mixture of both, but it seemed like the right thing to do overall.

"Perfect," Chloe said, "I'll see you tonight."

Betsy came around the counter and whispered to her, "I know we messed up. I'll make it right, ok?"

Chloe watched her walking away, wanting to believe that she meant what she said.

Chapter Five

In Which an Excuse Salad is Made

Chloe went home, admiring her purring truck. Why did it take a breakdown for one to appreciate the ease with which things usually worked? She walked in the door and was tackled by her dog. Today had been long to say the least, and she was as thrilled to see Marshmallow as Marshmallow was to see her. The chocolate lab spun around and jumped up on her again with all of her 80 pounds. Chloe staggered back, ruffling the dog's floppy ears. Her exuberance was relatable; it was difficult to hold back sometimes.

Chloe carried a tennis ball into the backyard and Marshmallow followed behind, eyes honed in on the ball. When they got into the back yard, she flung it as hard as she could and Marshmallow took off, retrieving it after the first bounce.

Now came the tricky part. Once the dog had fetched her quarry, she wouldn't give it up. Chloe ambled up to her at an angle, not making eye contact. She dangled a treat at her side and dropped it into the shaggy grass. The dog dove for it, letting go of the ball, which Chloe swiped up. They carried on like this for a little bit longer until one of them was ready for a change of pace. It wasn't the dog.

Chloe snapped on the leash and they headed down the driveway for their evening walk. The sun was already low in the sky when they set out. They passed some neighbors in their yards and waved before carrying on. A path intersected with the sidewalk and they turned onto it. It had been newly built, and the novelty of having a pedestrian path in their neighborhood hadn't worn off for either of them.

Marshmallow trotted along, enthusiastically tugging on the leash. She paused briefly from time to time to pick up a rock or sniff a tree. It was peaceful here. Chloe didn't pass anyone. She could hear cars passing on the nearby road, but the surrounding trees were dense enough that she couldn't see them.

She and Marshmallow made it all the way to the spot where the path ended at a cornfield. Topped with spindly tassels, the cornstalks were mostly brown now, with long, flopping leaves. Chloe flopped down as well. She stretched her legs out in the grass and closed her eyes. She rubbed her temples. It felt good to finally be still. Marshmallow sat next to her and set her head on her paws, sighing.

"You too, huh?" Chloe asked, leaning down beside her. She told her mostly faithful companion about every detail of her tumultuous day. Marshmallow looked up with her droopy eyes but didn't lift her head. A moment later however, she sat up tall and wagged her tail.

Chloe stopped talking. Someone was there. Why did people keep sneaking up on her? She glanced up a bit and saw a pair of running shoes on the path. They were attached to bare legs in basketball shorts. She looked up a little more to see a navy t-shirt below an unreadable little grin.

This was bordering on ridiculous. How did Arthur manage to creep up on her again? Maybe he hadn't been there that long. Who was she kidding though? Given how things had been going today, he'd probably been standing there the entire time. He had probably even heard her describing his square jaw and handsome face. Had he also heard her comment on how frustrating he was? She kind of hoped so. If he was going to bother people, then who was she not to say something about it?

He was still standing there, not speaking. She wanted to say, "Didn't anyone ever tell you to knock?" but she didn't. Partly because it didn't make sense in this context and partly because...well, the practicing restraint thing. Curse that restraint. "Hi. Out for a run?" she asked instead.

She waited. He didn't reply. Yes, she realized it was a silly question. Of course he was out for a run in his running shoes and his running shorts and his running t-shirt. He was sweaty and his face was red with exertion. But she was trying to make small talk. That's what people did. They made obvious observational comments to each other back and forth a couple of times and then moved on. Why did he refuse to follow the program?

"Yup," he finally said.

Ok... "Well, I better be on my way," she said.

He nodded and started to run back the way that he had come. Chloe stood up and dusted off the back of her shorts. She yelled to him before he was out of earshot. "I talk to my dog sometimes. Lots of people do that. I talk to my dog and I talk to my truck. Now you know."

He was fairly far away now, possibly out of range to have heard her. He called over his shoulder, "I talk to my cows all the time." He ran away and left her staring after him.

Who was this guy? He was some kind of stealthy ninja farmer was who he was. He seemed to think he was pretty hilarious too. Oh well, she happened to run into him twice today, but she never saw him otherwise. He might be at Hannah's wedding if the rest of his family was going, but that would be the end of it. And Chloe wouldn't do anything embarrassing at the wedding.

The rest of her family didn't come with that guarantee, but she would be on her best behavior. There wouldn't be any animals to talk to, and the only inanimate object she spoke with was Old Blue, who would be parked outside. It would be smooth sailing all the way.

She turned around to head home. Chloe's feet crunched on acorns, the fruit of the massive oaks that lined the path, and Marshmallow picked one up and chewed it noisily. When Chloe was a girl she had read that Native Americans used ground acorns for flour. That idea had appealed to her. They were everywhere, after all, and she admired their little caps.

She used to collect them under the oak in her backyard and smash them on the deck. They tasted awful, bitter and pasty. They had little holes in them. Not knowing where the holes had come from, she left them on her bedroom dresser. Worms emerged a few days later. Her mom lost her mind when she nearly stepped on the wriggling yellow grubs. That was the end of her acorn project.

She had since discovered that there was something one was supposed to do to acorns to them to make them edible. Check for holes, certainly. That would be a good start no matter what you did next. Then boil them maybe? She couldn't remember. Her dog didn't seem to have any objection to their taste, however. No boiling necessary. Marshmallow picked another one up in her teeth and split it with a pop.

Their other attraction, as far as her dog was concerned, was that they attracted squirrels. Fortunately for Chloe, there were no fluffy rodents in sight today, because once Marshmallow spotted one, all bets were off. She regularly broke away when a squirrel caught her eye during a walk.

When she got back home, Chloe paused on the sidewalk. Her home was a charming Cape Cod with an upstairs so tiny that it was almost a loft. She had been so busy this year, between gardening, building her business, and occasionally helping Lindsay at the bed and breakfast, that she hadn't done much with the flower gardens out front. They looked alright, if a bit wild. Perhaps she intended for them to look that way. They matched her crazy vegetable garden.

She ushered Marshmallow, who had discovered that she enjoyed the taste of the whirligigs beneath the maple tree as well, inside and went out back to pick tomatoes. She considered this year's garden to be a particular success. Squash and melon vines snaked between zucchini bushes before climbing up the wire fence that kept out rabbits and the occasional deer.

Tomato plants stretched up over their cages and arched their fruit laden vines. They were thriving and didn't seem to mind being sandwiched between the rhubarb and the bean teepee. She balanced on a stepping stone in the middle of the garden and bit into a cherry tomato. It popped, releasing its acidic juices. Was there anything like a ripe tomato in late September? The first frost would be coming soon, putting a swift end to the riotous jungle, and Chloe appreciated it all the more because of its ephemerality.

How she had lived for twenty-five years in Namur, Wisconsin, surrounded by farms, without learning to garden was beyond her. Once Bea introduced her to the joys of growing her own food, starting with a few tomato and pepper plants, she was hooked. She loved every part of the season, bookended as it was by the scent of warming soil in the spring and the bounty of the harvest in the fall.

Speaking of Bea, it was probably a good thing that she wasn't here now to see how out-of-control the garden had become. Bea was neat and meticulous and so was her garden, her vegetables lined up like soldiers in neat rows. Chloe's garden was more like a tangle of brawling rugby players who were all on the same team: the green one.

She wasn't in the garden long when Betsy came walking around the house.

"I'm back here," called Chloe. She had shifted her attention from the tomatoes to the beans, crouching beneath the bean teepee to pick a particularly long one that she must have missed earlier. Betsy wouldn't be able to see her in the wild twilit garden.

Chloe heard shoes padding over the grass. The garden gate creaked open.

"Hey, I'm here early," Betsy said. "Things were pretty much cleared out by seven, so Emma told me I could leave if I wanted to."

Betsy picked a tomato and tossed it in her mouth. No matter how often she did that, she never missed. If she had, though, it would've been alright because her work uniform matched the ripe cherry tomato. Her blouse was red with a curved collar, her apron decorated with a black and white checkerboard pattern. She smelled like melted butter and fried onions.

Chloe straightened up with her bowlful of veggies. "I was just picking things for our salad. See?"

Betsy laughed, not unkindly. "That's right. It's the special sister salad you wanted to enjoy with me."

"Ha ha. This salad is going to be awesome, and you'll be sorry for making fun of it."

Once inside the house, she rinsed the tomatoes in a colander and ran a couple of cucumbers under the water as well. She arranged them all on the cutting board and commenced chopping. Betsy leaned against the counter, clearly waiting for Chloe to give her the talking-to that she knew was coming.

Chloe nonchalantly cubed the veggies, not saying anything. She was probably being a bit mean, but she wanted her sister to stand there for a bit with her anxiety. Besides, it would give both of them a chance to think about what they were going to say so they could avoid a fight.

"I know that you know why I asked you here," Chloe finally said. "News of your antics is all around town."

"You mean you heard it from Karl, right?"

"Not necessarily." She focused on her vegetables.

"I knew it. Karl's always worrying about me. He's had a crush on me since we were two." She rolled her eyes again. "But yes. There was a scene, and I may have overreacted. Grace and I have been under a lot of stress lately. We thought it would help to go out and have some fun."

"You and Grace have been under stress? Stress from what?"

"I don't know. Like, Grace moved back up here to help her sister, and it's been a big change for her. And Dylan and I broke up recently."

"Was Dylan the one with the face tattoo or the one who scaled the water tower to spray paint your name on it?"

"He was neither of those...just..."

"Did it help? Relieve your stress I mean." Chloe tossed the veggies in the dressing and vigorously ground fresh peppercorns onto the salad. It was therapeutic.

"No. It didn't. Obviously."

"You and Mom need to stop rolling your eyes. It's not an attractive habit in an older woman."

"Speak for yourself. I'm not an older woman. Anyway, what happened was this: there was a group of guys there that we didn't know. They played a song on the jukebox. It was Sweet Home Alabama." She said the song title like it explained everything. And honestly, it kind of did. How had they known that Betsy couldn't resist Sweet Home Alabama? "They dared us to hop onto the pool table and dance. We thought it would be funny. I think you know what happened next."

Chloe nodded and sprinkled more pepper over the salad.

"You should stop doing that, or we won't be able to eat it," said Betsy, snatching the peppermill out of her hand and placing it out of reach on the counter. "I am so sorry. I'm going over there tomorrow to apologize to Ed. There's no way I'm going to even try to go back there again as a customer, ever. But I know I need to apologize. I'm going to offer to help out too. I'll do some cleaning or something."

That had been easier than Chloe had anticipated. And the notion of offering to clean was a good, if rather disgusting one. It was sure to win Ed over. The tavern showed no sign of having been cleaned since the 1950s, when his grandpa was the proprietor.

"Do you think Lindsay knows what happened?" Chloe asked.

"No. And please don't tell her. She's always worrying about Grace. I know you two are close, but Lindsay has so much to deal with. Steve is filing for divorce, and the bed and breakfast is really busy. I guess it stays busy until after October. Besides, Grace wasn't the one who threw her drink at Ed. That was me. I should deal with it."

Chloe was feeling encouraged. She wasn't thrilled with her little sister at the moment, but she had decided to take responsibility for what had happened on her own. That was progress. Credit where credit was due and all that.

There was still another issue to be addressed, though. "Are you going to stop going out so much?" Chloe asked. "It's not good for you to be out drinking every night of the week." It doesn't look good either, she didn't add.

"Yeah, I'll try. Last night was an exception. But it does seem like lately someone calls me almost every night after work to meet them somewhere." Betsy always was the popular one. "I agree that it's getting excessive though. If it makes you feel better, Grace is almost never out with us. She's usually at home with Lindsay. She just happened to want to meet me at Ed's after everything was quiet at the B&B."

"It does make me feel better actually."

Grace was sweet but impressionable. It would

be nice if Grace was the one doing the influencing instead of the other way around. It could still work out that way in the end, though. Even if Betsy went back to her old ways, Grace was almost certainly not going to. Like Betsy had said, she wouldn't want to upset Lindsay, especially not right now. This close call had most likely scared Grace straight.

Betsy was quiet for a bit. Chloe hoped she was considering the big turnaround that her life was about to take. She wasn't. "What about you?"

"What about me?" Chloe asked.

"It doesn't seem like you have as much fun as you used to."

"Mom said the same thing."

"See. Others are noticing it too."

"That proves nothing. I don't know where you two got the impression of me as a former party girl, but I don't feel all that different."

"Please, me in the present is nothing compared to you ten years ago."

"Do you really want to start this game? Because I guarantee…"

"Ok. No. You're right. But really."

"Well, going back to your question, are you talking about my kind of fun or your kind of fun? I don't have your kind of fun, because I don't want to get arrested."

"I have never been arrested."

"Not for lack of trying," Chloe said under her breath. She kept talking before Betsy could object. "But I am having fun. I've got my garden, my friends, my business, and my dog. What more do I need?"

"Yeah. I see that. But you used to go out more. You used to date. I'm not trying to be rude or anything..."

"Usually when you have to start a sentence like that, it's not wise to complete it."

"I mean it though. You asked me what I'm up to. I just wonder the same thing about you."

"I understand what you mean. I'm not interested in the bar scene anymore. I've grown out of it. But as far as dating goes, have you seen how that's gone for me? It's not anyone's idea of a good time. I'm a magnet for the wrong kinds of guys."

"Maybe the right kinds of guys are intimidated by you."

She waved the notion away. "That's just what people say when they have terrible personalities or bad breath."

"No, really. Look at you. You're beautiful and so smart. You make all these doohickeys." Betsy gestured to the papers and plans covering the table. "Maybe the right kind of guy is intimidated by you, and the wrong kind of guy isn't, you know? But what if a really sweet guy was interested in you?"

"If a really sweet guy just showed up out of the blue and asked me out, I would agree."

"See, that's so sweet. You deserve that."

"And then I would meet him in a public location and ask to look in his trunk. Surprise! He's in the mob. There's a body in there and a suitcase full of money. I'm on the run and have to go into witness protection. You never see or hear from me again."

"Oh my...just stop."

"Hear me out. This is important...where was I?"

"I never see or hear from you again."

"Oh yes. You never see or hear from me again until one day, in the far distant future. You're sitting on a train, pondering the days gone by when you used to have two older sisters instead of just the one. The good one, the one that you miss, has disappeared without a trace. You look out the window. Through the mist, you see someone on the platform. She turns around for a moment, glancing your way. She looks vaguely familiar, like a woman you used to know so long ago that it feels like a past life. Her head is wrapped in a scarf and she wears elegant sunglasses. At that moment, the train pulls away..."

"Forget I even said anything."

Chloe shrugged. "It's already been forgotten."

"I'm sorry I suggested such a dangerous path for you."

"Apology accepted."

Betsy picked up the salad and set it on the table amongst the papers. Chloe joined her with the salad tongs and some utensils.

"This excuse salad looks really good," Betsy said. She leaned over to smell it and sneezed. "It's a little peppery though."

Chapter Six

In Which an Unwelcome Guest Shows Herself Out

Chloe drove to Cedar Hollow Farm early the next morning. A hummingbird seemed to take residence in her chest as she neared the site of her breakdown. When nothing went awry, it flew away. She parked near the barn. No one else was there yet.

The sun was just coming up. The pastel colors of the sunrise were brushed across the horizon behind the barn, and there was a slight smell of rotting leaves along the foundation of the house where the breeze had collected them.

Chloe strolled through the farmyard. The hens were awake and strutting around her legs as she approached the back of the house. Bees clung lethargically to the asters that grew in the cottage garden along the fence line.

Chloe plucked a fat green apple blushed with red that clung loosely amongst crinkled yellowing leaves. Unlike the environs surrounding her apple tree, no rotting apples littered the ground here, making spidery wasps drunk on their fermenting juices.

Walking past the summer kitchen, she came

to the back door. She opened the screen door and knocked. Bea answered. She wore a floral apron and clutched her favorite turquoise mug, stamped with a honeybee. Chloe followed her inside. It smelled good in the kitchen, like caramelized sugar and freshly ground coffee.

"Coffee?" Bea held up a steaming pot.

"Yes, please." Chloe left so quickly this morning that she hadn't had anything to eat or drink. She may have suspected that there would be a spread as well. Bea handed her a hot mug, and Chloe wrapped her hands around it, taking in its full-bodied rich scent. Bea always made the good stuff. Chloe was less picky, but she appreciated quality coffee when she could get it.

Both women sat down at the table. "Is everything ok?" Bea asked.

Chloe examined her apple with great concentration. She wasn't the only one who could read her friends' minds.

"I was just thinking about Betsy," she said. "She got into some trouble a couple of nights ago. It was nothing awful, but bad enough."

"You'd settled down by that age."

"Why does everyone keep implying that I used to be like her?" Bea gave her a look and took a gulp of her coffee, arching one eyebrow. "Fine, I used to be a smidgen like that. But she's too old for this. I envy you. You don't have any sisters to worry about."

"I don't know. It must be nice, and you get to have two of them."

"There are some benefits," Chloe conceded. "But you have Harvey. When we were kids, I thought it would be fantastic to have an older brother looking out for me."

"Harvey did look out for me, that's for sure. He still does, actually. It bothered me when we were younger. I felt like he was hovering sometimes. Now I appreciate everything he's done. He really cares. But there seems to be something about sister relationships that's unique. Growing up with you and Lindsay was probably similar, but I'm not sure if it's exactly the same."

"I think it depends on the personalities involved. You and your brother have always been a lot closer than I am with my sisters. I honestly don't know what I would've done without you and Lindsay. How's Harvey doing anyway?" Chloe took a sip of her coffee as well. It was the perfect temperature, not so hot that it burnt her tongue but close.

"He's hanging in there. He's been over at Lindsay's, showing her how to maintain things that Steve had been doing before he left. She's learning a lot. Plus he's doing his forestry work, keeping up with his kids, and helping out on the farm a little. I've been trying not to ask for his help much though, given how busy he is."

"And how was your night with Wes? Weren't you two going to be swimming yesterday evening?"

"It was great and we did." Bea blushed behind her mug. "We made dinner over the camp fire. He even made a chocolate cake from scratch. It was incredible."

"You two are just too cute. And you were right. There probably won't be very many days left to swim."

The morning was chilly, and it wasn't supposed to be particularly warm today. Chloe looked outside. The huge maple by the barn was still green, but smatterings of red were popping up here and there, the first hints of what was to come. The weather in Wisconsin could go from summer to fall to winter in the blink of an eye.

There was a knock at the door and Bea answered it. It was Sarah and Lindsay. They came inside and   Bea glanced at the clock above the sink. It was almost show time.

"They should be here any minute. Should we go outside and start setting up?" she asked. She was in project mode now. "I put out some of your tools, Chloe. But I could use help carrying the food out to the picnic table."

Bea had crafted a beautiful breakfast of coffee cake and fruit salad, which they carried outside. Bea set a bowl of apples and a pitcher of milk in the center of a checkered tablecloth and the look was complete.

"Lovely," she said. "Now, we wait."

They sat at the picnic table, and Sarah told the rest of the women that her son George was coming back for a couple of months. Bea and Lindsay remembered him as well and said that they looked forward to seeing him again. Bea looked slightly wary, though. She was overwhelmed by Roy. Chloe guessed that the feeling extended to his son as well.

A line of cars started pulling into the drive-way, one after another. They were mostly trucks and Subarus with bumper stickers that said things like Crazy Chicken Lady or Farmers Feed Us All. In no time, all ten attendees were there.

Chloe recognized a few familiar faces and was thrilled to see that there were some new women here too. She visited with a few of them. Everyone seemed to specialize in something slightly different. Their interests ranged from candle making to hydroponics to llama husbandry. It was going to be a great group to learn from. Although she was usually the only one there who wasn't a farmer, Chloe always gleaned something that helped her, either in her garden or in her business.

Bea broke away from the group to make an announcement. "Thank you, everyone, for being here. If you're interested in helping out with the morning milking, feel free to follow me into the barn."

All of the women were interested, and they packed into the enclosure where the goats were milked. Bea demonstrated how she hooked the tubes up to each goat; she invited some others to try. Whether they were experienced or not, many of them gamely made an attempt.

When the goats had been milked, volunteers tried hand expressing the remaining milk, with mixed results. The ones who had done it before fared better than those who hadn't, but they all had fun. The goats seemed unfazed by all the attention. Every now and then they would look around them, vaguely curious as to what all the fuss was about, before going back to munching on their feed.

When they were finished milking, the women gathered around the picnic table where they would make formal introductions before Chloe demonstrated her farm tools. The first woman introduced herself as Carla. She ran an orchard in Fish Creek and sold fruits and vegetables at the farmer's market.

"My boyfriend Steve just moved up north to help out," she said. "He was from around here. Maybe you know him? Steve Thompson?"

What did she just say? Maybe Chloe had heard wrong. Lindsay's estranged husband was named Steve Thompson. He had left her, completely unexpectedly, less than two months ago. This had to be the same Steve.

Didn't Carla realize that he was recently separated? Chloe appraised her, standing there so innocently in her jeans and rolled up flannel, and guessed that she probably didn't. If she knew that she was dating a man who had just left his wife and was from around here to boot, she would know better than to announce it to a big group of women. Right? She didn't look crazy or evil, but Chloe had been fooled before.

Chloe was tempted to look at Lindsay to see if she was alright, but she didn't want to make her uncomfortable. From the frozen looks on the faces of her friends, Chloe could tell that they were thinking the exact same thing.

Lindsay held it together. She said, "Excuse me, I need to run into the house for a moment," and left.

Carla kept talking, as if the announcement meant nothing to her. She clearly didn't realize that she had just dealt someone a blow. Well, she'd know now. When she had finished speaking and another woman took her turn at introductions, Chloe sidled up to her and asked if they could speak privately.

Carla looked taken aback but agreed, following Chloe behind the summer kitchen to a clump of sumacs. Carla must have been appraising her as well. And she must not look like an axe murderer because this was actually pretty weird, leading a stranger behind a stone shed.

"I'm just going to cut to the chase," Chloe said. "It's about Steve, your boyfriend."

Now Carla looked truly alarmed. "What about him?"

"He's Lindsay's husband."

Understanding dawned on the woman's face, but she was unapologetic. "Her ex-husband you mean. I'm sorry. I didn't know, or I wouldn't have said anything."

"No. Not her ex-husband. Not yet. He left her without explanation two months ago."

"Two...two *months*?"

"That's what I said."

"That's not possible."

"Well it's true so..."

"But..."She stiffened and looked at Chloe like she didn't want to believe her. Chloe made a face that she hoped read: What reason would I have to be lying to you, lady?

"He told me they'd been divorced for two *years*."

"Nope." Chloe crossed her arms. She could keep going on like this for as long as it took.

"I met him about a year ago now and..." She trailed off, likely recalling inconsistencies in his story that seemed so clear in light of this new information. "I can't believe this. He seemed like such a nice guy. He said that she left him; he was heartbroken."

"Not a nice guy; not heartbroken." Chloe didn't want to cut this woman any slack. Taking in her stricken expression, however, led to the understanding that she had been hurt by this betrayal too. Not as much as Lindsay had, but a year was a long time to be with someone who turned out to have been lying the entire time.

She tried to soften the message. "I'm sorry you had to hear it like this, coming from someone you don't know."

"No. I'm glad you told me. I'm lucky in a way." She let out a mirthless laugh. "I may never have found out if I hadn't come here. I feel so stupid."

"Please don't. It could happen to anyone. And unfortunately, I can relate."

"He just rented a house nearby," Carla said. "He wanted to move in with me. I'm so glad I didn't go along with that. Maybe there was some part of me that knew something wasn't right. Please tell your friend that I won't be seeing him anymore. I truly had no idea."

"I'll pass that on to her. Thank you."

"If it's all the same to you, I'm going to sneak out."

Chloe had been busy considering how she would politely ask her to leave and was grateful that she thought of it first. There wouldn't have been a polite way to make that request. It was nothing personal.

"Again, I'm really sorry." Chloe said, trying to make up for her initial brusqueness. Carla marched back to her car, wiping her eyes with her sleeve.

Chloe stayed behind the kitchen for a minute. She was more outraged than astonished. This just confirmed what she'd been saying to Betsy last night. Dating wasn't worth it, marriage doubly so. You'd think you knew someone, and then one day they were leaving you a goodbye note and running off with a woman named Carla. Who needed it? Not her. What should she do for the time being though?

It was very likely that none of the other women had noticed that anything was wrong. Her best bet, the one that was kindest as well, was to rejoin the group and make sure that one of the members of the society went inside to check on their devastated friend.

This news couldn't have come as a bombshell to Lindsay either. She had suspected that there was something fishy going on, given that Steve had disappeared out of the blue. But to have it sprung on her like that, just when she was starting to get her feet under her again...

Chloe peeked around the summer kitchen to see what was happening. They were still talking and doing introductions; it didn't look like they had noticed that anything was amiss. It felt like half an hour had gone by, but it was likely only five minutes or so.

Pulling her head back, she looked up at the bright blue sky. The sumac leaves above her were changing along with the season, creating a canopy of spiky red leaves above her head. The leaves, clumped in neat intervals along the stem, looked almost tropical, their twisty limbs craggy and elegant at the same time. She pulled out a leaf and admired it in her hand. What had looked like a simple shade of red was really crimson fading to orange fading to yellow. How beautiful.

Ready to go back, she peeked around the wall of the kitchen for a second time. Sarah was gone, probably in the house. Good. Chloe would go back out and carry on with her demonstration as if nothing had happened. The last thing Lindsay would want was a scene. She had been anticipating this day more than any of them, and now it was ruined for her.

Steve deserved whatever consequences came from this revelation. It was a small world up here. He had to have been pretty arrogant to think that he wouldn't be found out. There was a very small bit of satisfaction that came from exposing him for the kind of person he was, but it didn't outweigh the disappointment she felt for her friend.

Chloe rejoined the group. No one, aside from Bea, seemed to notice that she had been missing. She listened to the rest of the introductions and then stepped up to the front of the group and introduced herself. She explained how she had gotten into making ergonomic farm tools for women and got the usual reaction. "This is incredible. I never thought about it that way before. This makes so much sense."

Now for the demonstration, they walked to an open field, each woman carrying a shovel in her hand. Chloe lived for the looks on women's faces when they first gripped the handles and dug into the earth with a shovel that was designed specifically for them. It might seem like a little thing, but to her it was everything. She knew that by the end of the day she would have multiple orders.

Bea took over next, leading the women to her beehives. That was Chloe's cue to slip away. She jogged across the grass and into the farmhouse.

Stepping into the kitchen, she heard voices coming from the living room. She hurried over to see Lindsay, slumped on the couch. Sarah sat next to her, patting her hand. Claudette, Bea's mom, was on the other side, speaking to her quietly.

Lindsay's head was down, but when Chloe came in she looked up at her from beneath her chestnut curls, which partially obscured her face. It looked like she had been crying, her eyes were red and puffy, but she wasn't anymore.

Chloe sat down on the chair next to the couch and Lindsay gave her a weak smile. "I'm glad you're here, because I know you'll understand. I just realized something. I'm not doing this. I'm not going to sit here and be sad today. Tell me all about it tomorrow. I do want to know the truth, even if it hurts. But today, forget it. Let's all go out there and finish this awesome day that we've been planning."

"Are you sure?" Chloe asked. "I'm up for it if you are, but you don't need to prove anything to any of us. We know how strong you are."

"Thank you for saying so, but I'm not doing it for anyone else. I'm doing it for myself." Lindsay stood. Another tear trickled down her cheek and she wiped it away. "That was the last one," she said. "For the next couple of hours anyway."

Sarah and Claudette stood up and so did Chloe. They followed Lindsay, who was already marching out the door towards the autumn sunshine, her hair illuminated like a glowing crown of autumn sumac.

Chapter Seven

In Which the Hunt is On

"Ok, we played pin the kisses on James Dean so now it's time for..." Betsy slapped a drum roll on her legs, "the scavenger hunt!"

She was beside herself with excitement. She had insisted on throwing their older sister a bachelorette party, even though Hannah had begged her not to make any kind of a fuss. In the end, Hannah agreed to the party, but only if Betsy kept the guest list small. Betsy had kept her word, only inviting their closest friends, but that was just about the only small thing about this evening.

Chloe, Bea, Hannah, and Grace sat in Betsy's living room. They were covered in confetti and wore toilet paper veils. Lindsay had been invited as well, but someone needed to stay behind at the bed and breakfast. Besides, Chloe guessed that she wasn't in the mood to celebrate the institution of marriage for the time being.

"A scavenger hunt?" Hannah asked. She rubbed her hands together. She loved a good competition. A scavenger hunt would be right up her alley. Chloe was impressed with how thoughtful Betsy had been about the games she chose. Their usually serious eldest sister was having a fabulous time.

"Surprise!" Betsy said. "It's a scavenger hunt around Namur. There are only a couple of rules: you can't leave town and you can't go to any private residences, including your own. We're going to split into two teams. When you find something on the list, snap a picture of it with your phone. You'll have two hours to find everything and get to Ed's Tavern." Betsy had been reinstated as a patron there already. After doing some serious cleaning, she had been forgiven. "If you haven't found everything within the allotted time, don't give up. Some of the things can be found at Ed's."

Betsy presented a list to each woman. It was printed on thick pink paper covered in swirly magenta type. How they were going to find all of these things in a town of 400, Chloe had no idea, but she was game for trying. They drew numbers to create two teams. Hannah and Bea were on one team, Grace and Chloe on the other.

"Now I'm going to flip a coin to see which team I'm on," Betsy said. "Chloe, you call it."

Given their excitement level, Chloe didn't know if she could handle Grace and Betsy together. She hoped that Betsy would end up with Bea. "Heads," Chloe said and heads it was.

Betsy cheered, not noticing the lukewarm response the news received. "Alright you guys. We'll split up and meet back at Ed's Tavern in two hours. You two can cross any three things off your list, because we have an extra player," she told Bea and Hannah.

They looked relieved, and Chloe could guess which ones would make the chopping block. She was sure that they didn't want to "get down on one knee and propose to a stranger" or "kiss a bartender" aka Ed, the only bartender in town. He was about as kissable as a burly sixty year old biker guy, which is exactly what he was. Was it possible that they were all going to be banned from Ed's tonight? The odds were 50/50 right now, but they could change as the night went on.

"On your mark," Betsy said. Everyone stood up. "Get set. Go!"

They jostled in the doorway and raced outside. Bea and Hannah hopped in Bea's van and drove off before the other three could decide whose car to take. Chloe laughed. The two members of the opposing team were the most reserved party guests, but they were also the most driven. They were going to be taking this competition very seriously.

And then there were her team members, who were skipping around Old Blue pumping their fists and chanting "Victorious Secret". That was quick. They had come up with a team name already.

"Looks like I'm the driver," Chloe said, opening up the door of her truck and waving them in. "Come on, Victorious Secret. They've got a head start on us."

Grace and Betsy squealed and both of them climbed into the back seat.

"You're going to make me be the chauffer?" Chloe asked. They were giggling uncontrollably back there. "Oh forget it. Let's go. One of you is going to have to tell me what we should find first, though. I can't read and drive at the same time."

Betsy snapped the list in front of her and read it in her official tone of voice. "I think we should attempt to find someone with the same name as the groom."

"Alfonse? You think we're going to find someone in Namur named Alfonse?" Chloe asked.

"Sure, why not? Let's go to the feed store."

"Because you think Alfonse needed to run to the feed store at seven o'clock on a Saturday night?"

"Chloe! I wrote these to be funny. Just go along with it."

"Ok, sorry. Let's go look for Alfonse at the feed store."

"Thank you madame," said Betsy, still being official.

When they turned onto Main Street, they saw Bea's van parked at Martel's Grocery. It looked busy there tonight.

"The grocery store. Curses! Why didn't we think of that?" Betsy shook her fist at the van, and she and Grace erupted into a storm of giggles again.

"Do you want me to turn in there too?" Chloe slowed down.

"No," Betsy said, waving her on. "We can't follow them. We'll come back later."

When they got to the feed store, Chloe stopped them before they could leap out of the truck. She swiveled around in her seat. "Do we have a plan? Are there other things we could cross off here?"

"Yes," said Betsy, scanning the list. "Let's find Alfonse and… take a picture in the men's bathroom."

"Fair enough," said Chloe. Better to check off the bathroom here than save that one for Ed's. "Let's go."

They strolled into the feed store. The clerk lowered his newspaper. It was almost empty in there. A couple of farmers were milling about amongst the bags of chicken feed and grass seed.

"Hi ladies, we're about to close any minute. Can I help you with something?"

"We're just browsing," said Grace.

She and Betsy were dressed in skinny jeans and heels, and Betsy's shirt draped off one shoulder. All three of them had some amount of toilet paper sticking out of their hair. That is to say, they didn't look like his average customers. The clerk nodded and went back to reading the farm report.

"Ok, let's split up and ask these guys if any of them is Alfonse," Chloe suggested. "Wait, how are we going to prove it, in the unlikely event that we find him?"

"We'll snap a photo of his ID," said Betsy. She had thought of everything. "Let's take a picture in the men's room first."

They walked to the back of the store and found it. There didn't seem to be anyone inside. Running in, they took a group selfie and dashed out. Betsy walked ahead of them and stood in the middle of the store. Before they could stop her, she cupped her hands around her mouth and called, "Is anyone here named Alfonse? We're looking for an Alfonse."

The clerk lowered his paper again. "What are you three up to? You can't be yelling in here."

No one else said anything. They looked up from their bags of feed for a moment and went back to shopping. One man, who carried a dozen farm fresh eggs, didn't even seem to notice that they were there. He walked up to the counter, and the clerk checked him out.

Chloe and Grace turned strawberry red and backed away from Betsy, but their ringleader was unabashed. She just shrugged and flipped her hair over her shoulder. "Huh. I guess he's not here."

"Let's go then," said Chloe, pulling on her sleeve. Chloe and Grace scurried out the door and hopped in the truck. Betsy strutted out behind them.

When they were all inside, Chloe made a request. "Can we please not make announcements in the middle of stores? We do have to live with these people after tonight."

Betsy craned her neck to check her makeup in the rearview mirror. She blotted a bit of lipstick at the corner of her mouth.

"What should we look for next?" Grace asked.

Betsy snapped to attention and scanned the list, considering. "Ooh, I have two good ones: ask an older couple for marriage advice and dance on a table."

Chloe spun around. "Dance on a table? That's one of them? Really? I thought you two learned your lesson."

"Dance on a table that's not at Ed's," Betsy clarified.

"Did you have someplace in mind that would allow us to do that?" Chloe asked.

"Emma's Café. It'll be perfect. We can grill Emma and Ernie for marriage advice, and I'd bet almost anything she'll let us dance on one of the tables if I ask her. She did help me plan this party, after all."

Chloe pulled out of the feed store parking lot, heading for Emma's. When the three women walked in, the waitress was busing a table.

"Have a seat, ladies. I'll be right over," she said. They slid into the booth by the front window, Chloe on one side, Grace and Betsy on the other. Emma sat down a moment later. Chloe had never seen her sitting down before.

"Are you doing the scavenger hunt?" Emma asked.

"We are," said Betsy, "We've only been to the feed store so far."

"This is such a hoot," Emma laughed. "Betsy and I have been coming up with ideas all week." Chloe pictured the two of them rushing past each other during peak breakfast time and murmuring, "Pose for a photo prom style" or "Get a lock of a guy's chest hair".

They had come up with some inspired ideas. Chloe hoped Bea and Hannah were having a good time too. It would be hilarious to see their pictures and hear about their parallel adventures around town.

"Which ones are you going for here?" Emma asked.

"We'd like to ask you and Ernie for marriage advice," said Betsy.

"Ooh boy, you've come to the right place for that one. We've been married for almost forty years and have worked together for all of them."

"Yikes," said Betsy. "I didn't know that. You're both still in one piece, so you must be doing something right."

"We have our little ways of making it work. Aren't you supposed to write this down?"

"A video will be even better, if that's ok," said Grace.

Emma smoothed the bun on top of her head, preparing for her debut. "I'm ready when you are," she said.

Grace held up her phone and mouthed, "Action."

Emma glanced over at the kitchen to make sure that her husband wasn't within earshot and said, "Pretend that you can't open the jar of applesauce." Grace wrinkled her forehead in confusion from behind her phone and Emma elaborated. "I'm a tough lady. I've worked here from morning to night since I was a teenager, and I'm not slowing down any time soon. But people like to know that they're needed. They like to know that you depend on them." She lowered her voice. "So sometimes, when we've been extra busy, and I've been running around here and running around at home, taking care of business, I pretend that I can't open a jar of applesauce. I ask Ernie to open it. It's a little thing, but I want him to know that I need him. He opens it and I say, 'Ernie, what would I do without you?' and he smiles; it makes my day."

"Wow. That's really sweet Emma. Thanks," said Grace.

"Also, marriage is like a pair of yoga pants. The most important thing is what you put in 'em."

Chloe clamped her mouth shut and tried not to laugh. Grace and Betsy nodded at this sage advice.

"We have to interview a couple. Can we ask Ernie too?" Betsy asked.

"Be my guest," said Emma, "but don't tell him about the applesauce."

They all agreed to keep it a secret and headed into the kitchen. Ernie looked up when they came back. He was in the middle of frying trippe in a pan. The cabbage sausages smelled amazing and Chloe was tempted to pilfer one.

"You ladies are looking fancy," he said. "What's the occasion?"

"It's our sister Hannah's bachelorette party. We're doing a scavenger hunt," said Betsy. "We need to get marriage advice from you. Emma already shared hers, so now it's your turn."

Ernie didn't hesitate. "Whatever she said is right. That's my advice."

"Wait," said Grace. "I didn't get that on video."

Ernie continued to flip the sausages. "Let me know when you're ready." Grace nodded. Ernie looked into the lens and said, "Emma honey, you're right." He laughed. "But seriously, my advice is to find someone you respect and who respects you. I admire Emma and the things that she stands for. That's the foundation for everything else."

Grace slipped her phone back into her purse. For some reason Chloe hadn't expected that level of depth from Ernie. She wasn't sure why. She had never really gotten to know him well, but his advice was really good. Who'd have thought? She'd write a book about it: life lessons learned during a bachelorette party scavenger hunt.

They thanked Ernie and walked back into the dining area. They sat down on stools at the counter.

"Are you going to ask her if we can dance on one of the tables?" Grace asked Betsy.

"Of course," she said. There were still a few diners present, all people that they knew. Betsy sidled up to her employer behind the counter. "Remember the one about dancing on a table?"

"Yes..." said Emma. She had to have known where this was going, but she was going to make her ask.

"Can we please dance on one of the tables?"

Emma looked between the scavengers and her little café tables. "Ok," she said. Betsy and Grace cheered, and Emma held up a hand so she could elaborate. "On two conditions: You need to take off your shoes, and only one of you at a time."

They raced over to a table, and Chloe waited for someone else to volunteer. They both looked at her expectantly.

"Me?" asked Chloe. "You want me to go first?"

They both nodded. Alright, here goes nothing. She slipped off her shoes and hopped onto the table. It wobbled a little and the other two stabilized it. Grace held onto it with one hand while extending the camera so she could snap a picture with her other hand.

"Here. I'll be the photographer," Emma offered.

Chloe swung her arms a little before hopping down. Grace did the same. When Betsy jumped up, the table teetered precariously. She danced with abandon, and Chloe stood ready to catch her if she tumbled off. The diners at the café clapped, which egged her on even more. Eventually, Emma helped her down and thoroughly sprayed the table while Betsy pulled on her shoes.

"Thanks Emma! That's three down, seventeen more to go," said Betsy. Two-thirds of the team whooped.

Once they were back in the truck, Chloe turned around in her seat. "Alright, what next?"

This time, Grace perused the list. "Bea and Hannah have probably left the grocery store by now. I think we can find some of these things there. Let's do 'hug a man with a beard', 'find something blue', and 'take a photo with someone in uniform'. We still have an hour before we have to meet at Ed's."

They arrived in no time and raced into the store. "Does Mrs. Martel count as someone in uniform?" Chloe asked.

Mrs. Martel presided behind the checkout

counter in her red apron, fluffing her curly white perm. She raised her eyebrows at them when they rushed in. She prided herself on staying abreast of everything that happened in town and had almost certainly heard about Betsy's gaffe at Ed's by now.

"On second thought," Chloe said, "let's ask Darlene for a picture."

Betsy and Grace agreed. Mrs. Martel's daughter Darlene was stationed behind the baked goods and was quite a bit warmer than her mother. Chloe reflected that it would be difficult to be bad tempered when a person spent that much time with sprinkled donuts. Darlene, whose bachelorette party days were long behind her, was thrilled to be part of the fun. They got a picture with her and continued on their quest, seeking a man with a beard and something blue.

They ran along the ends of the aisles, shooting a glance down each one. When they reached the freezer section, they found him. A man with a beard! It was Karl, debating the best ice cream flavor in front of the freezer. He reached for the mint chocolate chip, and Betsy ran to him, pinning his arms to his sides and nearly knocking him over.

"Karl!" she yelled. "Wait, we didn't get a picture of that."

Karl looked confused, but he wasn't about to question being hugged. Grace pulled out her camera, and Betsy repeated the performance, posing with one leg bent behind her. She kissed him on the cheek.

"Thanks Karl. We needed to hug a man with a

beard."

"Lucky me," he said. "What are you three up to?" They told him about the scavenger hunt. "Are you allowed to have help?" He held up his carton of ice cream. It sported a blue lid.

"Yes! Thank you," Betsy said, hugging and kissing him again.

Chloe thought she was kind of overdoing it now. Betsy and Karl posed with the ice cream, and Grace snapped the shot. She checked another item off the list.

"Gotta run," said Karl. "I don't want my ice cream to melt." He strolled away with an extra spring in this step.

"Let's go," said Chloe. "I suspect the proprietress is keeping tabs on us, and I'm not up for crossing her." The other two agreed and sneaked towards the entrance. Mrs. Martel wasn't at the register.

Once they were back in the truck, they considered the list again and agreed that they should head to the tavern early. It was late enough on a Saturday night that there would probably be a smallish crowd there. Most of these items were best suited to a bar atmosphere, anyway. They passed St. Mary of the Snows Catholic Church and pulled into the tavern parking lot.

The lots of the church and the tavern melded into each other. It was a matter of convenience, as it was a long-held tradition to meet at the tavern after Sunday morning service. Tom, one of the old men who could often be found telling stories on the benches outside of Emma's, had a pet theory about why there was a tavern next to every church in Southern Door County. Everyone would go to church and listen to the priest like they should, and then head over to the tavern to gab away about everything that they had been holding back during mass. Chloe thought his theory made sense, given how devoted people around here were to both their stories and their faith.

Inside the tavern patrons stood shoulder to shoulder, a group was playing darts, and some others were at the pool table. A crowd would help them blend in while they were doing all of the more awkward assignments on the list. It was noisy tonight too. A guy at the bar was loudly regaling his companion with a story, slapping him on the back for emphasis. When the man sitting next to him turned to see who had just come in, Chloe realized who the pair was: Arthur Watson and his newly returned brother, George.

Arthur looked like he was going to spin back around without acknowledging her, but George turned to see who had caught his twin's attention. He brightened up and called Chloe over to join them. She did, and he got up to give her his stool. Chloe was careful not to put her arms on the bar. Unlike the counter at Emma's, which was always pristine, the bar was sticky. The spots ranged from the obvious, like moisture rings from cold glasses of beer, to the unidentifiable, like what may or may not have been a moldy purple Skittle. Chloe glanced back to see if her teammates were still on the hunt. They had been distracted by a game at the pool table.

Now that Chloe was sitting next to Arthur, she wasn't sure if she had the nerve to go through with the rest of their game. Why did she let him rattle her? So he caught her at some dicey moments. Everyone has an off day sometimes.

Arthur was facing the bar and drinking his beer with that little grin on his face, and George had taken to slapping Chloe on the back now.

"It's been too long," he said. "What have you been up to?"

She told him about her business and its recent success. She might have exaggerated a little bit for Arthur's sake.

"Wow," said George, "I wish I would've thought of that. I think you've hit on something there. I've been investing in real estate. I've done alright, but what you've got going sounds brilliant, really brilliant. It takes a special kind of perceptive person to find a need and build a business around it. I'm trying to do the same thing myself."

Next to Chloe, Arthur quietly scoffed. The nerve of that guy! George was right. Her business was fabulous. "Thank you George. I'm very proud of the work I've done. It means a lot to me. Not everyone understands its significance, but not everyone can be a visionary."

Calling herself a visionary may have been a bit of a stretch, but she wanted Arthur to be on notice that she was passionate about what she did. Her efforts were valuable. If he didn't see that, it was his loss.

She turned away from Arthur to more fully face his twin. He looked like the kind of guy who would enjoy humoring a group of bachelorettes. "We stopped in because we're doing a bachelorette party scavenger hunt. Do you want to help us check off some of the tasks?"

"Are you kidding? I would like nothing better. Just tell me what to do, and I'll do it."

Chloe pulled the folded list out of her pocket. "You have quite a few options. You could serenade me with a Frank Sinatra song, we could tango, or you can give me your phone number on a napkin."

Without warning, George took her hands and struck a pose. She guessed that they were tangoing. He really seemed to know what he was doing, and Chloe went along with it. As he steered her past the pool table, she heard Betsy say, "Grace. Your phone." Grace started recording. George dipped her, making smoldering eye contact, and they crossed to the other side of the room. He started singing a Sinatra song at the top of his lungs as they danced. He had some pipes and knew all the words.

When George finished his ballad, he dipped her again. Everyone clapped and they bowed dramatically. He strode over to the bar, pulled a pen out of his pocket, and scribbled his phone number on a napkin. He handed it to Chloe and said, more quietly, "You really should call me."

She glanced at Arthur. He hadn't turned from

his front facing position on the stool during the entire interlude. He stared straight ahead, conversing with Ed every now and then. He wasn't even amused anymore, just disinterested.

Chloe had to hand it to George, though, he was bold. He was also exactly the kind of guy she would have fallen for in the past. Now, however, she was older and wiser and knew better than to actually call him. Thanks to her newfound wisdom, she could enjoy the excitement that he would inevitably bring to their sleepy little town and avoid heartache at the same time. She guessed those past mistakes had been instructive in their own way after all.

George sat back down next to his brother and carried on telling his story like he hadn't just had the full attention of the entire tavern. They looked almost identical, a country mouse and city mouse version of each other, but apparently that was where the similarities ended.

Betsy ran up to Chloe. "I can't believe it. You're basically carrying this team," she said.

"You can't believe it? I'm the middle sister. We are the most talented and amazing of all the sisters."

Betsy ignored that. She had something else on her mind. "Aren't you going to introduce me to your friend?"

As if she ever waited for an introduction. True to form, she wedged herself between George and Arthur and leaned against the bar, shooting George her most winning smile. "Hello. I'm Betsy, Chloe's *younger* sister."

"Nice to meet you." George shook her hand and introduced himself politely, not using the full force of his charm. He had seemed much more interested in Chloe and, based on the look on Betsy's face, that surprised both sisters equally. Betsy was the prettiest of the three sisters and could usually win guys like that over with a glance.

Betsy shrugged and walked away, whispering, "Apparently he's all yours," in Chloe's ear as she left.

Gee, thanks, Chloe thought.

Bea and Hannah walked in a moment later, brandishing their list triumphantly. "We got everything! Everything," Hannah shouted, grinning from ear to ear. The opposing team ran over to verify their win. There was a check mark next to every item.

"Ahhh! Congratulations you guys. This is too exciting." Betsy jumped up and down. She'd already forgotten about George.

"We weren't even close," said Grace.

Betsy vehemently disagreed. "We were still in the running. We just gained momentum late in the game."

"Thanks to Chloe." Grace nudged her. Chloe had to admit, she had been kind of amazing at the end.

"Want to go back to my house and check out each other's pictures?" Betsy asked. "It'll be half the fun."

"Just wait until you see Chloe tangoing with George." Grace wasn't going to let this go.

"Tangoing with George?" Bea asked, raising her eyebrows. Chloe shrugged. What could she say? Apparently was still capable of spontaneity every now and then. "I would love to see that. Let's go."

George and Arthur were still talking at the bar, but George gave Chloe a wink as she headed out the door. Yup, pure trouble. She winked back though because, why not?

Chapter Eight

In Which Wedding Preparations Hit a Snag

"You are a lifesaver." Lindsay shimmied up a ladder propped against the wall of her barn and hung an autumn wreath. "Your sister's wedding will be gorgeous. It's my first really big event here since...well, you know, and I really want it to be a success. Every little win helps me believe that I can do this."

"You can absolutely do this, and I'm thrilled to be helping," said Chloe. "This place is great. I can't believe that it was ever a tumble-down old barn."

"I've been here every step of the way, and I can't either. I have big plans for this place."

"You sold me already. I'm in."

Lindsay laughed. "Well, that was easy. I'm really planning on holding all kinds of events. Steve used to do odd jobs, handyman stuff, around town to compensate for our slow season. Now that he's not here, I need to come up with more ideas myself. You already know about the Halloween party. I'm considering having one for New Year's too."

"I love it. Please let me help. You've done so much to make this place look fabulous, it would be a travesty not to use it."

A huge wagon wheel chandelier sparkled above their heads. Antique lanterns dangled from its spokes by metal chains. The October day was brisk, but inside the barn it was warm and cozy. Chloe stepped outside to grab metal pots of reed grass, and Lindsay called to her from inside the barn.

"Just a second," said Chloe.

When she walked back in, Lindsay was setting up the arch. Chloe set down the pot. "I'm here. What's up?"

"Can you check my phone?"

"Of course, where is it?"

"I think I left on the on the back porch. Just see if they left a message. It could be one of the vendors. The chairs were supposed to be here first thing this morning, and there's been no sign of them. I would grab it, but if I let this thing go it's going to fall over."

"Will do," Chloe said. She ran up the stairs that led to Lindsay's kitchen. Her phone was perched on the railing and, sure enough, there was a message.

"Hi. Lindsay? This is Brian with Quality Rentals. I'm so sorry, but we double booked your event. The items you ordered six months ago are already spoken for. We won't be able to deliver...let's see... 150 cream white chairs to your location today. Rest assured that we will be offering you a refund and three percent off your next purchase. Have a nice day."

Chloe stood there, rooted to the spot. What could she do? How was she going to tell Lindsay that she was short 150 seats? She was just saying how important this event was to her, and now no one would have anywhere to sit. That seemed like a pretty important detail. Chloe sneaked into the house and sat down at the kitchen table. She stared at the phone, willing it to provide a solution. Could she call someone?

She sunk her head into her hands, trying to think. What could they use for chairs? They could gather up the kitchen chairs of every person they knew. That would look awful, but at least there would be seating. Lindsay was so particular, though. It was part of what made her events so spectacular. The chairs needed to match. They needed to look rustic or wedding-y or something, and they needed a whole gaggle of them by tonight.

What did they have a lot of around here? They couldn't sit on cows, although that would certainly be memorable. What about...straw bales! Yes, they could use straw bales. Chloe had seen it in a magazine. A couple had a rustic outdoor wedding, and they had straw bales lined up in a row for the ceremony. They would look perfect in the barn too.

She called Bea, who answered on the second ring.

"I'm so happy you're there."

"Chloe? What's going on? Isn't this Lindsay's phone?"

"I'm at her house getting ready for the wedding."

"Oh that's right, I remember you saying you were doing that. Do you need help?"

"Yes. I need a lot of help, actually. I need 150 bales of straw."

"What? Why?"

"The guy who was supposed to bring the chairs just called and said that they're not coming. Lindsay doesn't know yet. I wanted to come up with a solution before I told her. She's been working really hard to make everything perfect."

Bea was quiet on the other end. "Did you need 150 chairs? You should be able to fit two people to a bale of straw."

"You're right. Ok, so we only need 75. That seems more reasonable."

"I agree. I can bring some, but I don't have 75 bales. Hmm...let's ask around. I have an idea. Tell Lindsay that you need to pick up something for the wedding at my house and come over here. We can load the straw and stop at some neighbors' houses to see if they have any we can borrow. They should still be usable after the wedding. I bet lots of people would be willing to lend them for a couple of nights."

"You're the best. Thank you. I'll be over in ten." Chloe left the kitchen. Back in the barn, Lindsay was placing the grasses on either side of the arch.

"I have to run over to Bea's," said Chloe. "She said she has something for us, something for the wedding."

"That was nice of her. Did she say what it was?"

Chloe hated to lie, but it was for a good cause. "No. She just said it was something indispensable for the wedding to be complete."

"Wow. Do you want me to come with you?"

"Nope. You stay here. I'll be right back."

Lindsay continued decorating, and Chloe scurried away. When she got to Cedar Hollow Farm, Bea was waiting for her outside surrounded by straw bales. Her face was red and she was covered in straw. "I have 30 here, but we're not going to be able to fit them all in the van, and it's not nearly enough. Let's go over to Arthur's and see if he can help."

Chloe wasn't sure if she wanted to see the grinning, scoffing farmer again, but she'd do anything to help Lindsay and make sure that Hannah's wedding went off without a hitch. She and Bea drove over in Old Blue. He wasn't outside, so they walked up the porch steps. They were flanked by pumpkins. A pretty antique apple crate next to the door was topped with the pot of yellow chrysanthemums. Bea rang the doorbell. He didn't answer.

Chloe looked around. "I'll go check the barn," she said. Bea stayed there in case Arthur was slow getting to the door. Time was of the essence. They didn't want Lindsay to get suspicious and call either one of them before they were sure that this plan was going to work.

Chloe found him in the barn, standing at the workbench with a saw in his hand. "Hi," she called out. She, for one, didn't sneak up on a person when he thought he was alone.

Arthur looked up "Oh. Hey."

Chloe knew that a brief greeting would be the extent of their pleasantries, so she started right in on telling him what had happened.

When she had finished, he said, "I have enough to supply the rest of them, and I have a big trailer. It would have to be pulled with the tractor, though. Lindsay's house isn't too far from here, right? It's the bed and breakfast?"

"Right. So you can do it?" It looked like they were going to have seating after all.

"Yes. Definitely. Just help me load the straw bales. I'll meet you over there."

"Oh thank you, thank you. This is fantastic. I'm going to go tell Bea." Chloe turned around and almost ran into her. She was already standing in the entrance to the barn.

"Does this mean we have the rest of the straw?" Bea asked.

"Yes," said Chloe. "Arthur saved the day."

Upon hearing that he was the hero of the moment, he smiled a real smile, not just a grin this time.

They formulated a plan. The two women would assist Arthur in loading his trailer then he'd drive to Bea's farm to pick up the rest of the straw bales. Now that things were falling into place, Chloe felt confident enough to call Lindsay and tell her what was going on. She didn't answer, prompting an image of Lindsay's phone on the kitchen table inside. Oh well, she would be extra surprised by the trailer full of straw bales.

The bales were massive and heavy, making them cumbersome to move. Arthur stood on the trailer and Bea and Chloe hoisted them up to him.

When they were all loaded, the women drove back to Cedar Hollow Farm in Old Blue. Arthur followed with his tractor. They threw in Bea's straw bales and Chloe and Arthur agreed to meet at Lindsay's. Bea needed to stay back at the farm, but would be there tomorrow for the wedding.

Bea stopped them before they left. "Chloe," Bea said, "do you have plans before the wedding tomorrow?"

"I have to be there a little early, but I don't have any plans other than that. Why? Did you have something in mind?"

"I did. Do you want to come over for brunch at Wes's cabin before we go? Let's say around 9:30."

"Sounds perfect," she said.

"You're going too, right?" Bea asked, turning to Arthur.

"Yes, I'll be there," he said.

"Would you like to come over as well? We can drive over together, you and Chloe and Wes and me." Chloe wondered if her friend was up to something.

"Sure. That would be great," said Arthur.

"It's a date then," Bea clapped her hands together and walked back into the barn. Now Chloe knew that she was up to something. Was she trying to set them up? Oh well, it was only brunch. Maybe she was just being neighborly.

Chloe drove back over to Lindsay's in front of Arthur's puttering tractor. She soon outpaced him and arrived back in time to see Lindsay coming out of the barn just as she pulled into the driveway.

"So, what was Bea's surprise contribution?" Lindsay asked.

"It's on its way. It's actually related to the call you missed earlier. They left a message. It was the rental company that was supposed to be delivering the chairs."

"Supposed to be? What do you mean? I just called them and they didn't answer."

"The chairs aren't coming..."

"What?"

"The chairs aren't coming, but we came up with a solution."

"What's the solution? I'm panicking here. Where did you find one hundred and fifty chairs?"

"We didn't. Not exactly. Arthur's on his way with 75 straw bales."

"Straw bales? For seating?" Lindsay asked. Chloe got nervous. It had seemed like a brilliant idea moments ago. "That's fantastic. They'll look amazing in the barn. Thank you for thinking of it."

Well, that was a relief. "Any time. That's what friends are for, right? Supplying emergency straw bales?"

"Yes. They're also for not telling me in advance that I wasn't going to have any chairs. I'm trying to keep a brave face, but I don't know how long I can keep doing this without Steve."

"You're doing an amazing job."

"Issues are coming up every day, though. This is just one of many. I've had more customer complaints lately. It's been difficult to be as meticulous as I used to be, and people have come to expect high standards here. Sorry, I really appreciate your help. I'm being such a downer lately."

"Hey, I'd rather hear the truth about how you're doing than have you sugar-coat it. You're in a difficult situation that you had no time to prepare for. Please keep asking for help."

"I don't want people to think I need rescuing..."

"None of us would think that for a minute, so put it out of your mind." Arm in arm, they went back into the barn and continued setting up. Lindsay had finished almost everything while Chloe was gone. Pumpkins and gourds decorated the periphery and grapevine wreaths laced with real leaves, dried berries, and acorns hung from the walls. A matching garland wound through the chandelier.

"Does this look like the barn of a person who needs rescuing? No. You just need backup." Chloe did her Rose the Riveter move. Finally, a chance to break it out.

The rumble of a tractor outside clued them in that the seating had arrived. They ran out to see Arthur, a knight on a green steed, coming up the long dirt driveway.

"You have no idea how much this means to me," Lindsay called to him. "Not having chairs would've been a disaster."

Grace must have heard the tractor as well. She bounded out the back door. "That's a lot of straw," she said. "Are we setting up a straw bale maze?"

"We're using them as seats for the wedding

guests tomorrow," Lindsay explained.

"How perfect." Grace offered to help, and everyone unloaded the bales and hauled them into the barn. They lined them up in neat rows with an aisle down the middle.

When they were finished, they all stepped back to appreciate the effect. "These look even better than those plastic chairs would have," said Lindsay. "I might have to switch over to straw from here on out."

Arthur started walking back to his tractor, but Lindsay stopped him before he was out the door. "I was about to heat up some fresh pressed cider. Would you like to stay and have some? I'll bring it out to you," she said.

"Cider sounds great."

The two sisters went inside and Chloe sat down on a hay bale. Arthur perched on the one directly across the aisle from her. He was silent, but for once it didn't bother her. His assistance in saving the wedding had gone a long way to helping her see him in another light. Now that she gave him a chance, Chloe found that he was a comfortable person to be around, when she wasn't preoccupied with appearing foolish in front of him. He wasn't grinning at her now; he was admiring the festive surroundings.

"Lindsay's going to be holding events here more often," said Chloe. "She's determined to make it a big success."

"What kinds of events?"

"More weddings. Maybe concerts too, and parties. She's having one for Halloween and thinking about one for New Year's. The whole community is invited. You should come."

Arthur looked taken aback. He must not be used to receiving multiple invitations in a day. In Chloe's limited experience, he was a guy who kept himself to himself. She was pleasantly surprised when he said, "I'll be there. Thanks."

"I was saying to Bea the other day that it's funny that we haven't gotten to know each other at all, with you living so close to her," she said. "And now this is the fourth time we've run into each other in a month." Not that she was counting... "I wasn't doing anything too peculiar today though...unless you count my request of forty bales of straw. I guess that's kind of odd."

"I don't think you're odd at all..." he said, rubbing his neck. He was about to say something else when Lindsay walked in carrying two mugs of steaming cider.

She handed one to each of them. "I have to run back into the house to do a couple of things, but you two can feel free to stay in here as long as you'd like. Don't forget to pick some apples for your apple butter, Chloe. You should take some too," she said to Arthur. "And again, thank you. You two have no idea how much all of this means to me." She took in the straw bales, completing the picture of a perfect fall wedding site, and tears welled up in her eyes as she walked away.

Chloe tried to take a sip of the apple cider, but it was scalding hot. She was tempted to power through, but knew that she would pay the price of a burnt tongue if she did. She stirred it with a cinnamon stick and decided to wait. Looking up, she realized that Arthur was watching her. He glanced away and took a sip from his mug.

"Ah!" he said. "That's really hot."

"It's hard to wait though. I've been struggling with it myself. Do you want to take a walk in the orchard while it cools off?"

He did. The noon sun peeked through streaks of lofty clouds and the air was crisp and cool. Most of the apples had been picked the month before, but there were a few that still hung on, along with some dry yellow leaves.

"Have you always farmed?" Chloe asked. "I mean, I know you grew up on a farm, but did you always know it was what you wanted to do?"

"Yes. I loved it from the start. I worked with my brother on our family farm until I saved up enough to buy one of my own. I couldn't believe my luck when the property I ended up with came up for sale."

It was a beautiful spot. The view from his front porch featured a wildflower meadow edged with cedars that hid Wes's cabin in the woods. The only evidence that the cabin was there was the windmill that peeked out of the trees.

"Have you always designed farm tools?" he asked.

"No. I was an engineer at a boat factory up north, but it wasn't my passion. And then I discovered gardening, and I learned about how so many things, farm tools included, are designed for men. Women have learned to adapt, but it's not ideal. So then it came to me...Sorry, I get a little overzealous when it comes to my tools."

"It's great. I admire your enthusiasm. I feel the same way about farming. It's all I've ever wanted to do. It's never boring. There's always something new to learn."

"Exactly, and every time you learn something new, another avenue of discovery opens up to you. One thing leads to another. It's incredible."

She sipped her cider. It was finally cool enough to drink.

"And you have your society, right?" Arthur asked.

She nodded. "We do.When it started, it was just Bea and me, but we had big dreams. We called it the Demeter Society right away. Demeter's the Greek goddess of agriculture. We like to think of ourselves that way too." She smiled up at him and he laughed. "And then Lindsay moved back, your mom joined, and the rest is history. What about you? Is there a secret competing society of men farmers?"

"There is. I'm not allowed to talk about it though."

"No way!"

"I'm kidding."

"Aww. I kind of liked the idea of having rivals."

"Well, I really am a member of a society of sorts, but I'm going to keep you in suspense about it until tomorrow. You'll see at the wedding."

"A society of mysterious wedding crashers, I like it. I'm looking forward to it."

"I am too."

They strolled the length of the apple orchard. The unceasing October breeze turned their cheeks ruddy and pink and tilted the craggy apple trees in one direction. Chloe was cozy in her Irish sweater and the cider kept her hands toasty warm, but the tips of her ears were growing a bit numb.

Upon their return, Chloe picked up a basket that had been conveniently left out for her. She passed one to Arthur as well. She scoured the orchard for the less attractive apples. "I have a theory that the ones with blemishes taste better," she said. "If the bugs were willing to take a bite of them, they're good enough for me."

"Makes sense," Arthur agreed. "I thought I heard something about apple butter."

"I make it every year. Lindsay gives me free reign to pick as many apples as I'd like with the stipulation that I'll bring her a few jars."

"I love it too, but I never have enough patience to let it get really thick. Mine just ends up being apple sauce."

"I'm not usually winning at patience either, but it's worth it. I'll make some tonight and bring you a jar at the wedding tomorrow. You can share it with the members of your secret society."

"I'll have to keep it concealed from them. One of our tenets is that we can't eat apple butter."

"Ok. Now I know you're kidding."

"Maybe, maybe not," he said.

Chloe silently thanked Bea for her meddling brunch plans. She'd get to see Arthur right away in the morning again. Wait. How had she been so obtuse? Lindsay was in on this too. Cider in the barn? Apple picking? Two baskets left out in the autumn grass? She could think of no finer friends.

Chapter Nine

In Which Arthur Reveals a Hidden Talent

Not having set foot in Wes's cabin since he moved there in July, Chloe couldn't believe how different it looked from what she had imagined when they went there as kids. It hadn't been occupied then, and it looked forlorn and spooky. There had been gaps between the logs and some of the windows had been broken.

Now, its inhabitants were protected against the morning chill by new windows and solid walls. Flames danced in an ornate woodstove in the corner. Wes's uncle cleaned it up and replaced many of the original elements, but nothing stood out as being new or out of place. He had fine taste.

The only things that did look out of place in the rustic setting were the people seated around the table. Chloe wore a crimson bridesmaid's dress. Its twisted straps crossed in the back and its flowing skirt hung to the floor. The matching shawl, it was the middle of autumn after all, featured an intricate pattern laced with gold.

The embroidery matched her flaxen hair, which was twisted into an elegant low bun. Her mom had begged to style it, but Chloe wasn't interested in waking up at the crack of dawn to spend hours in the salon just to end up with Lego woman hair.

She had put in a good effort though. She even wore a stunning shade of red lipstick for the occasion. Her mom and sisters would approve. When Chloe had teased them that she would show up in her work boots, they hadn't been amused.

Bea stood at the counter, pouring herself another cup of coffee. Her brown hair was up too, in a French braid that wrapped around her head. There was no sign of the famous grays that she had been worrying about. She had chosen an emerald gown that brought out the flecks of green in her hazel eyes. When she and Chloe stood together, they looked like they were preparing for Christmas already.

Wes looked at ease in a suit, of course, with his trendy glasses and casually rumpled hair. He was telling Arthur the story of what happened when he came back to town after over a decade away. "My friend Hugh helped me move back and hardly anyone saw him, but he kept doing all these funny things. Everyone ended up thinking that I was making him up."

"I think I remember hearing something about that," Arthur said. "Hugh sounds a lot like me, wild and unpredictable."

Was he joking? He was joking. He had that familiar little grin again, but he sat stiffly, clearly unaccustomed to being so dressed up.

He noticed Chloe appraising him and said, "I'm usually covered in camouflage and have been sitting in a tree for four hours by this time on a Saturday."

Bea agreed. "I don't think people realize what a big compliment it is when hunters attend their weddings on beautiful fall weekends."

"I guarantee that Hannah doesn't," said Chloe. No one in her family hunted, least of all Hannah. She tried to picture her in a deer stand and couldn't. She would be reading a book and would've forgotten to bring a gun.

"That's alright, we're just teasing," said Bea.

"Speak for yourself," Arthur joked. They laughed and Chloe added deer hunting to the list of things that people took seriously around here. "Have you gotten anything yet this year?" Arthur asked Bea.

"No. Not yet. My dad shot a little doe. Between Harvey, my dad, and me we usually get two or three and share the meat among us. Harvey makes venison jerky. What about you?"

"I got a buck, but I'll keep trying. I end up passing a lot of it on to my parents too. My mom is an expert at cooking with venison, and I know she likes to have some every year. My dad hunts, but he's not always as patient or quiet as he could be. That's another thing I get really excited about," he told Chloe, referring back to their conversation in the orchard yesterday. "I turkey and pheasant hunt too."

Chloe considered that Arthur probably would have had time to have gone hunting this morning if he hadn't agreed to come to brunch. She may not have been a hunter, but she was not insensible to what a compliment it was that he had chosen to be here instead.

"I'd love to try hunting some time," she said. She had developed the interest just now.

"You should come with me. It's really peaceful, and I usually see something. Even if I don't see any deer, I'll see a fisher or even a bobcat. The other day, a chickadee landed on my bow."

Chloe imagined sitting in a deer stand with Arthur. She could've stayed there around the table with the delicious food for hours. No such luck.

"Sorry to run, but I have to leave early," she said. "We're going to do a walkthrough of the ceremony before the guests arrive."

"I have to be there early too," said Arthur. She looked at him in confusion. "For my society, remember? I told you that you would find out about it today."

Chloe remembered. But what could his society have to do with Hannah's wedding?

"Do you want to drive together?" Arthur asked her.

"I'd love to. Is it ok if I leave my truck here, Wes?"

"Of course," he said. Chloe's truck was parked next to the Door County Bookmobile, which Wes was keeping at his house for the time being. Old Blue would feel like a youngster compared to the 70 year old mobile library.

Chloe wrapped her shawl around her shoulders, and she and Arthur said goodbye. Bea and Wes went back to talking, sipping their coffee and smiling like they couldn't believe their luck.

They had been apart for twelve years before finally realizing that they should be together. If Chloe took that path, she would have to find someone and be tragically separated from them. They could come back together in their forties. Given how well any of her other approaches had worked, the scheme as worthy of consideration.

As she followed Arthur outside, she remembered something. "I made you apple butter. Just a second." She ran to her truck and came back with two mason jars full of rich brown sauce.

"This looks incredible. I'll probably eat it right out of the jar."

"Go for it. I won't judge," she said. He held the door open, and she climbed into his truck. As they drove she asked, "Can you give me a clue about your society?"

"Sure," he said. "We're not a group of women farmers."

"Ha ha," she said. "Well there go all of my guesses." They pulled out onto the county road and passed his farm. The four pumpkins that had been lined up on the steps had turned into jack-o-lanterns overnight. "Did you carve all of those?" she asked.

"I did. Well, not just me. My oldest brother, the one who runs our family farm, has three kids. They came over last night and we carved pumpkins. It's a tradition. I have a pumpkin patch especially for my nieces and nephews. They get some to carve and then they sell whatever's left over for some fun money. We have a bit of a competition going now that they're older, and they make some really elaborate designs. I'm still a triangle eyes and nose and a toothy grin kind of a guy."

Chloe was speechless. Was he for real? There had to be something wrong with him. She was checking the bed of his truck for that body and suitcase of money the second they arrived at the farm. If nothing turned up, then she had to consider the possibility that his society was a group of guys who hate dogs. Or maybe they taxidermy chipmunks and dress them up as historical figures so they can reenact famous battles. She saw a documentary about people like that once.

"Do you have a dog?" she asked.

"I don't. My last dog, Daisy, was the best though. She showed up on my farm as a raggedy little puppy and never left. She grew into a big fluffy golden retriever. It was like she knew she belonged with me. She followed me everywhere. I still think I see her out of the corner of my eye sometimes."

He smiled and shook his head, remembering his old friend. "I haven't had the heart to get another one since she passed away last year. I saw your dog, but we were never formally introduced. She appears to be a good listener."

Chloe laughed. "She is. Her name's Marshmallow. She's a big lug but I love her. I got her from a shelter last year." So he loved dogs...on to the next thought. "Are you into taxidermy at all?"

"No. Not really. Are you?" he asked.

"Nope," she said. She wasn't giving up. There was something going on here.

When they got to Lindsay's, there were quite a few cars parked along the road, but no one was outside. "I'll meet you in there," Arthur said. "I have to grab a few things."

"Do you need help carrying anything?" Chloe asked. Any briefcases full of unmarked bills?

"No thanks," he said. "I'll see you inside." He reached behind the front seat. This was it, the moment when the horrible truth would be revealed. Chloe tried to peek, but he was waiting for her to leave, probably so she wouldn't be implicated in whatever nefarious activities he was involved in. That was thoughtful. She reluctantly walked to the barn, stealing a few backward glances.

The wedding party, minus the groom, was gathered around the arch listening to the pastor. Chloe scooted over and joined them, trying to blend in. She hadn't thought that they were running late, but everyone else seemed to have been there for a while. She sidled up next to Hannah.

The pastor walked them through the ceremony, where they would stand and what he would be saying at each part. "The musicians will be setting up next to the stage, so why don't you all wait outside? Once the music starts, we'll make sure our pace is right and that you're in the correct order."

They stood outside and waited until the musicians were ready. They must have gone in the back door. Chloe hadn't seen them enter, but she could hear them warming up. All of the women were bouncing up and down, wrapping their shawls around their shoulders. The men, on the other hand, were warm and comfortable in their tuxedoes.

Ah ha! She had another moment of realization. Here she was, shivering and balancing precariously on pointy shoes, while the men donned flat wide shoes and cozy jackets. What would her sister have done if she had shown up in a tuxedo? She'd consider that at the next event here. Halloween was coming right up. She knew she was supposed to be a sexy nurse or a sexy barmaid or a sexy...anything really. Instead, she would rock a fine yellow banana costume. The thought made her happy.

Chloe considered the groomsmen. Were any of them a likely candidate for an outfit swap? It was difficult to say. Her dad cut quite a fine figure in his suit, and her mom looked lovely as well, if a bit showy. Her low cut dress was gold and her thigh peeked out of a big slit up the skirt.

The music began in earnest. It was Pachelbel's Canon, of course. The most overused song in wedding history. So why were her eyes stinging like she had never heard it before or paid attention to its beauty? Was she becoming sentimental? Not a chance. "Not sentimental" were her two middle names. Could that be Arthur's secret? Maybe he was a hypnotist and was messing with her mind. She didn't feel like herself at all.

She tried to ignore the music and lined up with the other women. Betsy turned around, squeezed

Chloe's shoulder in anticipation, and stepped forward. Chloe waited until her sister was halfway up the aisle before starting down herself. She clutched her bouquet at her waist and took measured steps, teetering on her high heels. She mimed Betsy, who strode up the aisle with elegant ease, but wasn't able to match her poise. She looked at the string quartet; at the people who were playing such affecting music.

There was Arthur, drawing the bow across the strings of a violin. He swayed to the music, focusing intently on the sheet in front of him. He looked up at her for a moment and grinned before continuing to play.

That was his secret? He played the violin? That wasn't creepy at all. That was amazing. Chloe couldn't believe that farming, hunting, straw bale heaving Arthur was playing this beautiful music. She slowed, trying to take another step while still keeping her eyes on him, and twisted her ankle, tumbling over onto the floor. There was a collective gasp and the music screeched to a halt.

She popped up, stumbled a little, and brushed off her dress. She leaned over to pick up her bouquet, which looked a little worse for the wear. Lifting her hand, she shouted, "I'm ok, everybody. Carry on." Betsy tried to maintain her composure, but tears were streaming down her face. Chloe started laugh-crying too. Once one of them started laughing, the other couldn't resist.

Their mom yelled from the open barn door, "Stop goofing around you two! You're going to wreck your makeup." After some mumbling from her dad, she added, "And it's your sister's big day."

Chloe and Betsy composed themselves with much difficulty and walked the rest of the way down the aisle. The musicians started up again as if they had never been interrupted. Chloe stared straight ahead and lined up with the other bridesmaids. Once she was safely stationary, she stole another peek at Arthur. He was completely engrossed in his music again.

When everyone was at the front of the church but the bride, Arthur and his fellow musicians switched over to the wedding march, and Hannah followed with their dad. Chloe had never seen her looking so radiant before. She was statuesque, at least a head taller than Chloe, and her long sleeved lace gown was sleek and elegant. She smiled so confidently, without a trace of trepidation, that Chloe had to conclude that she and Alfonse stood half a chance. Hannah gave both of her sisters a hard glare before taking her place at the front.

"It's a good thing we had a practice run," the pastor said, smiling. Chloe appreciated a man of the cloth with a sense of humor. She agreed. Apparently she had required a practice run.

Chapter Ten

In Which Parts of the Evening Were Best Forgotten

The second time Chloe strolled down the aisle, she didn't stumble. She might have glanced at Arthur a couple of times, but she had practiced walking in her heels by trotting around the barn beforehand. She was quite proud of herself and stood triumphantly at the front of the church. Her future brother-in-law cried when he said the vows that he had written, and Chloe struggled to keep it together for the second time that day. She was going to have to do something more in character during the reception in order to make up for these lapses.

When dinner was served, Chloe found herself between her mom and younger sister at the head table. It was almost as if Hannah had foreseen that Chloe would do something embarrassing on this momentous occasion and crafted a cunning punishment beforehand. Her table companions argued past her. They were discussing a recent Hollywood breakup between two people that Chloe had never heard of. Her mom adamantly supported one party while Betsy championed the other with equal passion.

Apparently this thing was so significant to both of them that they stopped speaking halfway through the first course. That suited Chloe perfectly fine. She couldn't have planned it better herself. To ensure that the feud would simmer at least until dessert, she whispered to both of them in turn, "You are so right. Don't ever back down."

Arthur sat at a table with his "society". They talked and laughed nonstop throughout the meal. He caught Chloe looking at him and smiled. She smiled back.

She sensed the danger of this situation and wasn't sure how she felt about it yet. It was so easy to resist someone like George, because men like him were familiar territory. They were fun for a while and then one or both of them would get bored and move on and no one would get hurt. Or that was how it worked in theory anyway.

Chloe must have grown out of that arrangement, because she had to admit that she had been hurt more than a few times. The problem with a guy like Arthur, then, was that he seemed like the kind of person that she could really come to care for. She didn't like to confront her vulnerability. She felt more comfortable going into situations where it was easy be deluded. Maybe she was getting ahead of herself though. Arthur wasn't necessarily interested in her. He had just accepted a couple of invitations from her sweet meddling friends. Nothing significant had happened, yet.

"What are you thinking about?" Betsy asked.

"Nothing," said Chloe. "What do you mean?"

"You're staring at that guy."

"What guy?"

"Oh my gosh. Why are you staring at that guy?"

"I have no idea what you're talking about." *So stop talking about it.* Chloe didn't want her mom to hear a peep about her being connected with anyone, especially not anyone that she was maybe possibly interested in.

"That's Arthur, right? That's George's twin. They were at the bar."

Chloe glanced around a while, as if she didn't know his precise location, before she let her gaze land at his table. "Sure, I suppose that's him." She turned to Betsy. "I wasn't staring at anyone though."

"Well, that's funny, because 'anyone' is getting up from his table and walking this way."

"What?" Chloe whipped around to look again. Arthur sat there, oblivious to the fact that they were talking about him.

"And...you totally gave yourself away," Betsy hummed, looking way too proud of herself, and any guilt that Chloe felt about stoking the flames of her feud with their mom evaporated.

Betsy went back to eating, but her gaze flicked between her sister and Arthur. She would be watching them like a hawk for the rest of the evening.

Chloe was about to take another bite of steak when her mom clinked her wine glass, commanding the attention of the entire room. Her mom loved giving speeches, and Chloe wondered aloud how long it take their dad to pulled on her dress to get her to sit down.

"I give it five minutes," said Betsy, already on it.

"Three," Chloe replied.

"Wow. Big expectations."

"Please, I'm being generous. She's been on a roll lately."

"Who hasn't?" Betsy asked as Chloe surreptitiously started the timer on her phone under the table.

"Thank you so much everyone for being here. I'm Tammi, the mother of the bride. Can you believe it? I look so great, right? We get mistaken for sisters all the time. But it's true. Little old me gave birth to her 32 years ago. She's the first of my girls to get married. They've all been dragging their feet to the altar. Not that they haven't had a good number of gentlemen callers over the years, am I right ladies?"

Chloe checked if the tablecloth reached the floor. It could act as cover for her to escape from the prying eyes of every single person they knew, plus their new in-laws.

Her mom paused to polish off her glass of champagne. It had only been one minute. How had she successfully accomplished so much in such a short period of time?

"Her dad and I have been married for 31 blessed years. We couldn't be happier. You do the math, right?"

Wow. Her husband was tugging on her already, and she had barely hit the two minute mark. She swatted him away and carried on. "I guess I'm needed elsewhere, but the most important thing I wanted to say is that I'm thrilled to welcome Alfonse to the family. I know that he will make our precious daughter very happy." She sat back down.

That last part had been alright. It was quite nice actually. People usually only remembered the end of speeches anyway. Chloe made up that little truism on the spot as a bit of consolation. Wait. It wasn't over. She was getting back up.

"If Hannah's as much of a cougar as her mother, Alfonse will be a very happy man as well." She smoothed her dress around her hips and shimmied before sitting back down for good this time.

Chloe banished her first consoling thought and considered that maybe no one had been listening. She had been so focused on her mother's train wreck of a speech that she hadn't looked out at the assembled guests. She turned to face them. They stared at the head table in shock. Conversation had ground to a halt. George pumped his fist and whooped, and the people around him laughed. Chloe silently thanked him for cutting through the tension as everyone went back to chatting and eating.

She leaned past her mom to look at Hannah and gauge her reaction. The bride was talking and laughing with her groom, unperturbed. That was one benefit of being so unflappable, Chloe supposed. Hannah went with the flow and shrugged off her family's idiosyncrasies. She also lived three hours away, which had to have been a calculated move. Maybe Chloe didn't give her enough credit. She made an appearance every now and then, let the craziness roll off her back, and then left unscathed.

The other speeches were appropriate if forgettable. The cake was delicious-a pumpkin spice and vanilla affair made by Lindsay. The DJ arrived right on time. Chloe helped Lindsay bus the tables and scoot the straw bales to the edge of the barn, clearing the way for a dance floor. The bride and groom had the first dance, but by the second song, half the attendees were out there doing the chicken dance.

Chloe would join them soon, but she needed to rest for a moment first. She sat across the length of a straw bale along the wall, propping up her legs and dangling her feet over the edge. George's voice boomed from behind a gaggle of women who were blocking her view.

"I hear you showed up here with Chloe," he said.

"I did," said Arthur. "We were at Wes Jacquemart's cabin for brunch. We both needed to be here early, so we drove over together."

"A brunch? It sounds like there might be more to that story," George chuckled. "Come on, you can tell me."

"There really isn't. She's a fun person. I hope we can be friends, but I'm not interested in her like that at all."

Chloe, who had been slouching, sat up straighter now. She should've known. Arthur didn't have a deep dark secret. That's why she hadn't stood a chance with him from the beginning. She wasn't heartbroken or anything. He had only started to not irritate her precisely one day ago, but she had to admit that she was disappointed. He seemed like a great guy and he probably was. Go figure.

"So you don't mind if I ask her to dance?" George asked.

"Knock yourself out."

"You have to admit, she's not bad to look at."

"Sure, she's pretty enough. Her eyes are an interesting shade of blue."

"Her eyes? That's all you've got? Ok, I believe you. You're not interested. So who's the lucky lady then?"

"There isn't one. I'm perfectly happy on my own."

"I'll never understand how you can live in this puny town all alone on that little farm."

"I wasn't always alone…"

"Let's just drop it."

"Happily."

Arthur didn't sound happy at all. It was reminiscent of her conversation with Betsy. It must be a sibling thing. Oh well, she would have at least one dance with George. That would be entertaining. The two men moved on in the knick of time. The cluster of women had drifted enough to deprive her of their cover.

She was about to get up when Drake slid up next to her. The fog of scent from the pomade in his slicked back hair descended on them instantly. "So, which one of you lovely ladies is going to be next?"

"I'm sorry, what?" She wasn't in the mood for conversation, least of all with Drake.

"Your oldest sister is married now. That clears the way for you and Betsy."

Why did people keep saying that? What was this, 1810?

"My money's on you," he said. "I'm shocked you haven't been snapped up already." He ran his hand over his hair then fiddled with the bottom button on his suit coat, leaving behind greasy fingerprints. He always left that bottom button open. It drove Chloe crazy.

"You wouldn't want to dance, would you? I just got promoted at the bank, you know."

A promotion at the bank? In that case, sign me up. "Congratulations," she said. "I would love to dance, but Bea's calling for me."

He wrinkled his brow and tilted his head, listening for a moment. "I don't hear her."

"She's right over there." Chloe pointed at Bea. Fortunately, she was looking at them. She waved for Chloe to join them at the table. "We have a very complicated code that we use to communicate. See, she just blinked three times." She blinked at Bea a few times. Bea gave her a confused look but then shrugged and went along with it. Friends understood when a person had her reasons.

"Oh yes," said Drake. "I just saw her blink as well. How interesting."

"I'll be right over, Bea. Sorry, gotta run." She hopped up and trotted over to the table. "If anyone asks, we have a complicated communication system. It's Morse code with blinking."

"Got it," Bea said.

"You can stop trying to set me up with Arthur, by the way. He's not interested." Bea started to object, but Chloe interrupted her. "I'm onto you and Lindsay. We've had pre-wedding brunch with another couple and drank hot apple cider on a crisp fall day in a rustic barn, all within the span of 24 hours."

"Yes. Fine, we were trying to set you up," Bea said.

"Ah ha!"

"You seemed like a perfect match."

"Didn't we though?"

"I know! And, although your tango with George was dramatic, we thought that Arthur seemed like a better fit for you. When I say that out loud, it sounds like we're being really meddling."

"It's alright, I understand the impulse. Arthur also has the advantage of being less like the guys I usually date. It was kind of a no-brainer."

"Exactly. Thank you".

"Were you trying to distract me from George, then?"

"A little bit." It was difficult to see someone you love make the same mistakes over and over again. "Why don't you think Arthur's interested though? You two seemed like you really hit it off this morning."

"I thought so too, but then I overheard him talking to George. He said that my eyes were alright, but he wouldn't touch me with a ten foot pole."

"He did not say that."

"That was the spirit of the thing."

"Oh, I'm sorry."

Chloe shrugged. "Don't be. It's not like we were engaged or anything. I appreciate that you were thinking of me. Apparently finding a normal guy with no weird issues isn't in the cards for me. George and I may have an encore performance, though, so watch out for that. And Drake's trying, again."

Bea laughed. "Aren't you two related?"

"Distantly, but apparently that's not enough of a deterrent for him."

"Well I'm sorry for interfering with you and Arthur. We had good intentions."

"I know you did. I get it. And honestly, my one day with a nice guy was special. I'll always remember it as a shining moment in a sea of bad breakups, weird relatives, and histrionic arguments. Sorry, I'm getting dramatic."

"Bea knows dramatic, and that's not it," Wes chimed in, smiling. He could be a bit dramatic himself. It was part of what made him so endearing. "Do you want to dance?" he asked them.

A new song had come on and he led them onto the dance floor. They maneuvered around a couple of groomsmen who were flailing their limbs every which way and a toddler who spun like a top with her arms outstretched. They found a somewhat clear space to dance.

Wes had some good moves. So good, in fact,

that before the song was over, a circle had formed around him. Bea joined him and they danced a while before rejoining the crowd. George filled the vacancy at the center of the circle next and grabbed Chloe's hand.

Once again, she marveled at his ability to not only dance well but to make her feel like she could too. She was so lost in the moment that she didn't notice when the tempo changed and a slow song started. George held out his arm and she took it.

"Where did you learn to dance like that?" she asked.

"I've been taking ballroom lessons for a few years. It keeps me out of trouble for the most part."

I bet it doesn't, Chloe thought. He had the exact same dimple as Arthur.

"What about you?" he asked. "You're pretty good yourself."

"No I'm not. I was just mimicking you, but thank you for saying so."

"So your business keeps you out of trouble."

"For the most part," Chloe said.

"Speaking of business, I have a proposal that I think you might be interested in." He twirled her around. "I know this is really last minute, but I had plans with an investor tomorrow. We were supposed to kayak around the Cana Island Lighthouse, but his plans have changed, and now he can't make it. Would you be interested in joining me?"

She considered. Was he interested in talking business with her as well, or was this a date? If it was a date, the answer was going to have to be no. She was determined not to go there.

Picking up on her hesitation, he clarified his intentions. "I'd like us to discuss what I was planning on discussing with my potential investor. I'm interested in developing retail space and apartments at the site of the former library. Your business sounds like a perfect fit for that location."

"You think so? I hadn't thought about having a shop yet."

"I see people like you all the time. You're fantastic at design but you have no head for business, right?"

"Guilty."

"Well, that's where I come in."

Chloe was a bit uncomfortable with the idea of using the space where the library still stood, because she hadn't wanted to see it demolished. On the other hand, it was going to be gone whether she was involved or not. She could at least hear him out. It was supposed to be a beautiful day tomorrow. If nothing else, it would be an adventure.

"I really think you should consider it," he said. "It sounds like your business is taking off. A store would give you visibility. You would develop stronger customer relationships. It would allow people to test your products in person."

He was really trying to sell it. Those were all good points, though. "I'll need to consider it some more."

"Of course. Tomorrow will be totally informal.

We'll be kayaking and hiking and stuff. I'll just lay out a few ideas and you can see if they stick. If it turns out that it's not the right fit for you, no harm done."

She liked the sound of that. No pressure. "Alright. Let's do it."

"Great." He looked thrilled, and Chloe hoped she wasn't getting his hopes up for nothing, unsure if she could even afford retail space yet.

"I'll pick you up at eight," he said. The song ended and he thanked her for the dances and walked away, greeting some old friends from across the room.

Chloe was parched. Her feet throbbed. She had enough of her pointy shoes. She went up to the bar and requested an ice water. As she was coming back, she spied all of the members of the Demeter Society, plus Arthur and Wes, seated at a round table. She pulled up a straw bale and joined them.

Chloe guzzled down her water. "What a party," she said to Lindsay. She slipped her shoes off under the table, hoping no one would notice.

"I don't want to count my chickens before they've hatched, but I think we might've pulled this off," Lindsay said. The dance floor was still packed. George was dancing with Betsy now. He was the one trying to keep up with her this time.

Arthur got up and sat down next to Chloe. She scooted over to give him more room. "So, what did you think of my society?" he asked.

"You were all incredible," she said. "You made me fall over."

"I've never had that happen before. I'll take it

as a compliment."

"You should. How long have you been playing?"

"Since I was eight. As a kid I was always humming and tapping out tunes on the table. My mom started me with an instrument so I wouldn't drive everyone crazy. It kind of backfired on her for a while though. If you've ever heard a novice violin player, you know what I mean."

"Well you play beautifully now."

"Thank you. It feels a little cliché, a fiddling farmer, but my chickens like it so it comes in handy."

"So you talk to your cows and play music for your chickens. That's a lively little farm you have there."

He laughed. "I was meaning to ask you, do you want to try hunting with me next Saturday? It's the rut so we should see a lot of deer."

"I don't know what that means."

"It means the boy deer are trying to impress their girlfriends."

"Sounds exciting."

"It is, but I go early so I understand if you're not up for it…"

She didn't have to consider whether or not to accept this invitation. "I'd love to." It was just what she needed: spending time in nature with a nice normal guy. Even if he was only interested in her as a friend, she really liked him. He was interesting, helpful, and kind. He was also easy on the eyes. What more could she want?

"Great. I'll pick you up at six," he said. "You're lucky. It gets dark late this time of year."

Six is late? Yikes. "You know what though?" Chloe said. "We need to consider something. There seems to be a direct correlation between the number of times I see you and my level of zaniness. Even I'm left wondering what I'll do next, and I'm guessing a tree stand is not a place for nonsense."

"Well, you'll be strapped in up there. I think it would be difficult for too much zaniness to happen."

"You'd be surprised." They both laughed.

"I'm looking forward to seeing what you can manage."

Chapter Eleven

In Which George and Chloe Traverse Storm-Tossed Waters
(Not to Worry: George is a World-Class Swimmer)

It is a truth universally acknowledged that a rogue in possession of good looks can't help but use them to his advantage. Chloe and George stood before a lineup of kayaks. They looked small and flimsy in contrast to the vastness of Lake Michigan. The sky was pewter gray and towering clouds rolled in from the west. Waves crashed onto the shore incessantly, creating a dull roar.

Apparently three layers of clothing were not enough to keep out the October chill. A young man with an ironic curly moustache unhooked two of the kayaks and handed a paddle to each of them.

"Are you sure this is a good idea?" Chloe asked him, strapping on a life vest.

"You'll be fine," he said. "You can pull onto shore anywhere around the island if the weather turns nasty." It really wasn't a matter of if, but when.

"Don't worry," George said. "I'll rescue you if you fall out. I'm a world-class swimmer." He pulled off his glasses-why he wore sunglasses on an overcast day like this, she wasn't sure-and polished them on his undershirt, revealing chiseled abs. He caught her looking and grinned.

Chloe smiled thinly. She wasn't comforted by assurances about his swimming prowess. She also wondered if he was planning on keeping his shirt on today. Had agreeing to this outing been a mistake?

She thought back to her mom and sister, accusing her of losing her adventurous spirit. Were they right? Had she become too cautious? No. Not Chloe. Adventure was her middle name. Bring it on stormy Lake Michigan. Bring it on roguish gentleman barely pretending not to flirt. She could take on both of them.

Shoving her kayak as close to the edge of the lake as she could manage without getting her shoes wet, she hopped in. The mustachioed man pushed her into the water with a bon voyage and then did the same for George. They were off.

The waves insisted on pushing them back to shore, but Chloe found that as long as she continued to paddle she was able to make some forward progress. George zipped ahead of her and she picked up the pace, not wanting to be left behind. Arms burning and eyes stinging, she propelled herself forward, not giving up.

They rowed parallel to a sandy causeway that connected the island to the shore. On calmer days, one could walk out to the island that way without getting wet, but today passage by foot would've been impossible. The sandy berm emerged every now and then only to be swallowed up by the lake once more. They would likely have the entire island to themselves once they moored their boats and hiked to the lighthouse. No one else would be foolish enough to even attempt the voyage.

The white lighthouse tower could be seen from shore, rising above the cedars. The keeper's house was hidden from view, but glimpses of its roof could be seen through the trees. Water sprayed Chloe with every wave she crested and she gradually became soaked. When they neared the shore of the island, however, the water became calmer, the paddling much easier.

She drifted next to George and they both glided along, letting their paddles rest across their laps. "I'm not sure that I can do much more of this," said George, shaking out his arms. He lifted them over his head and stretched back, exposing his stomach again. Chloe willed herself to look straight ahead.

"I'm so glad you said that," she said, "because my arms feel like rubber too."

"Do you want to pull onto shore right here instead of going all the way around the island? We can head to the lighthouse and warm up inside."

Chloe happily agreed. Getting here had been the difficult part. She wouldn't want to repeat that experience. Now that they had almost arrived, however, going back would be a piece of cake. They'd be working with the waves instead of against them.

They pulled their kayaks onto the shore and then yanked them up even farther to be certain that they wouldn't wash away. Chloe's feet squished into the sand as she pulled. When they reached the grass, they both agreed that the waves were unlikely to make it all the way there and left the kayaks where they lay.

"I apologize for the intense workout after our festive night," said George. "It was a great time but I stayed out way too late."

"Me too, but don't apologize. This is amazing." She couldn't remember the last time she had gone on an adventure like this. Now that they were safely on the island, the clouds looked more beautiful than menacing.

"Want to run for it?" she asked, edging towards the cedars that ringed the island. A single raindrop plopped onto her head. The clouds were almost upon them now. The weather was sure to get worse before it got better.

Chloe didn't have to ask twice. George took off running and she sprinted after him. They bushwhacked through the trees until they reached the mowed yard that surrounded the lighthouse. As they stepped out into the open, they realized that the rain had, in fact, picked up considerably. By the time they ran across the lawn and bolted into the brick house, they were dripping wet. They startled the docent, who was sitting on a stool in the gift shop, sipping a cup of tea.

"Oh my! I didn't think anyone would be coming out today," she said. "You two are soaked! Did you swim here?"

"Very nearly," Chloe replied. "We kayaked here. I'm not sure if we'll be able to take the same mode of transportation back." Rain battered the window and streaked down in rivulets. They had made it just in time. It was exhilarating.

"Have a seat," the woman said, gesturing to a table in the next room. They headed into the kitchen and George sat down. Chloe skirted the room, examining the built-in cabinets that covered one side of the wall. Original dishes were on display here, thin white plates and soup bowls and a simple porcelain pitcher, as well as food canisters from the early 1900s. Canning jars and a metal flour sifter sat on open shelving down below. A battered white sideboard, which must have held silverware and linens at one time, abutted a matching stove.

Chloe plucked a pamphlet off the sideboard and pulled up a chair at the table across from George. "It says here that the lighthouse was built in 1869 and is still in operation. Huh. I didn't know that it was still running. Did you see a light on the way here?"

The docent returned with their tea. "There's no keeper here anymore. Everything is automated, but the light automatically turns on at dusk and off at dawn." She set the cups down in front of them. "The tower isn't open for tours today, but you can visit the history rooms upstairs. Look out for the ghost though; he's especially active when it's stormy." She turned to walk away.

Not so fast. "A ghost? You're kidding, right?"

The woman spun around and hurried to sit

down with them. She must have been anticipating Chloe's reaction, because she started in on the story right away. "I didn't believe it myself, not at first anyway. I know full well how people like to tell tales about these old places. But then one day, there was a terrible storm. Usually the hay wagon is able to take us across the causeway at the end of the day, but that evening it was decided that it would be too dangerous to cross at all."

"I've heard about the wagon," said Chloe. "A tractor pulls it across the causeway when the water's too high to cross on foot, right?"

"Precisely," the woman said, "So, it was determined that it would be safer for me to stay the night. I was a little nervous, to be quite honest. It's one thing to scoff at ghost stories in the light of day, but quite another when one is stuck on an island in a storm overnight."

"So, did you end up seeing the ghost?" Chloe couldn't wait to find out.

"Not precisely. But I may have heard him."

"Do tell," George said.

"Like I said, I was concerned about staying here overnight alone, but I wasn't left with a choice. Besides, there were ample comforts left here for me. We're stocked with supplies in the event that one of us has to stay: toothbrushes, soap, a bit of food. I planned to sleep in one of the upstairs bedrooms, the former keeper's room.

"That night, just as I was falling asleep, I heard loud clanging footsteps on the spiral staircase leading up to the lighthouse tower. I was afraid to move at first, but eventually I mustered up my courage and looked inside the tower. It's encased with metal now, which is what you see from the outside. Inside, however, it's revealed that it's really made of brick, like the house. It's crumbling a bit, but the brick should have muffled any sound, even if someone was jumping on those stairs. I climbed all the way up to the top of the tower, and never saw a soul, living or otherwise.

"When I got to the top, I looked out over the lake and I could have sworn that I saw something moving over the water, heading in the direction of one of the shipwrecks. I ran down the stairs and hid under the covers until morning."

"Has anything else happened since?" Chloe asked.

"Not that night, but now that I'm more open to it, I will admit to noticing strange occurrences. For instance, they were doing some restoration on an outbuilding next to the house, and every now and then someone on the crew would come in, saying that a tool had gone missing. I didn't know anything about it, of course, but later it would appear on a shelf here in the kitchen or on one of the beds upstairs."

"And you think it was the ghost?" Chloe asked.

"I can't say for sure...but I've been here long enough to be inclined to think that, when it comes to this lighthouse, there's more than meets the eye." The woman left, but she had thoroughly convinced Chloe to check out the upstairs. She loved ghost stories. Besides, there was something so romantic about the idea of a lone lighthouse keeper, maintaining a steady beam of light that shone out into the frigid lake to keep sailors from crashing onto the shoals around the island.

The docent popped back in. "Would you like anything else? We have pear scones today."

They both said that they would love a pear scone and were soon sipping tea and dabbing buttery crumbs from the corners of their mouths. Kayaking in a storm was hungry work. "So, do you think we'll run into the ghost today?" George asked. "Don't worry, I'll protect you."

Oh please. "I would love to see a ghost. And you're the one who shouldn't fret. I'll be protecting you."

"Why am I not surprised? Do you want to talk business now, or do you need a little more time to recover from our voyage?"

"Let's talk business." Chloe pulled off her raincoat and draped it over the back of the chair. "I'd love to get a better idea of what you're envisioning."

"I've been talking to investors and there's a lot of interest in this property. Even though the town is so small, it's the entryway to Door County, so it'll get decent foot traffic from spring to fall."

"Do you have any plans drawn up?" He came around the table and sat down next to her. Scooting his chair close, he reached into the pocket of his coat and pulled out a big plastic bag which protected a large piece of parchment. He unfolded it between them. "I've been working with an architect for a couple of months and this is what we've come up with."

She wondered if he had starting planning this before or after a decision had been made about the library. He walked her through the plans. "There would be space for two businesses downstairs. I'm trying to attract operations that reflect the character of the area somehow. A farm to table restaurant or a market that carries local produce would be ideal for one of the stores. And for the other shop, I would love to see you here." He pointed to a spacious shop on the first floor.

Not having had much time to consider any of this before crashing into bed last night, Chloe didn't know how invested to be in this vision yet. But while she was getting ready for the day this morning, she did imagine what she would want her store to be like. She wouldn't have to limit herself to just selling tools in a space that large. She could sell books about all things agriculture as well as clothes, bags, and jewelry made by other women-owned small businesses. Her success would help promote other women's endeavors.

"The apartments upstairs will be eco-friendly. We're planning on installing solar panels on the roof, using rainwater collection to supply water for our rooftop garden, and setting up a site for composting. We're also researching carbon neutral and sustainable building materials and will be using them wherever it's feasible to do so."

"This sounds incredible. What's the catch?"

George laughed. He looked her in the eye and moved closer. "There is no catch. I've been involved in the development of quite a few properties like this in Minneapolis and they're thriving. They were a bit larger, but the basic principles are the same."

"So what's next?" she asked, scooting back to put a little more space between them.

"I'll be in touch about the details. I like to know in advance if business owners are interested."

"I'm interested for sure," Chloe leaned across the table, inspecting the plans but then sat back. She didn't want to appear too eager. "It's something I'll strongly consider. I need to look into a few things, but I'd appreciate it if you'd keep me posted."

"Great." George folded up the plans and put them away. He pushed back from the table and stood up. "That's enough business talk for now. Do you want to go upstairs?" He raised one eyebrow and grinned.

He was too much for Chloe not to grin back. They climbed the narrow stairs to the bedrooms. Faded ivy wallpaper, peeling at the corners, decorated the keeper's room. A narrow bed covered in a faded quilt was pushed up against the center of one wall and a wooden dresser stood along the wall opposite. It smelled musty and unlived in here, but there wasn't a speck of dust on anything. Chloe looked out the window. Rain continued to pour down in sheets.

The door creaked behind her, and she turned around just in time to see it snap closed. The glass doorknob wiggled, almost imperceptibly. She strode across the room, startling when she caught her reflection in the wavy mirror above the dresser. When she reached the door, she tried to pull it open. It felt as though someone was holding it closed on the other side.

"George?" she called quietly. "Is that you?"

No response. Letting go of the doorknob, she tiptoed across the room, avoiding the mirror this time. She didn't believe in ghosts, but an antique mirror in a closed room on a blustery October day was best avoided. She hid behind the bed and waited.

The door creaked again, opening this time. Chloe peered under the bed, watching George's hiking boots as he stepped gingerly across the wide floorboards. When he had nearly reached her, she popped up with a shout.

"Boo!"

George almost jumped over his own head. "I can't believe I didn't see that coming."

"You have to wake up pretty early in the morning to fool me."

"I really thought I had you, too." George had let his guard down for a minute, losing his arrogant sneer in his fright. He recovered quickly however, and pulled her into the other room. "You have to see this," he said. "This bulb is the size of my pinkie."

"Is that the light that shines out of the lighthouse tower?" It looked like a slightly oversized bulb from a string of Christmas lights.

"I guess it is. Apparently it can be seen from over 15 miles away."

A sign next to the bulb said that a prism surrounding the light amplified it so that it could be seen from great distances. Next to the individual light was something that looked like a gear with more bulbs poking out of it. There were multiple bulbs in the tower, and this gadget allowed the keeper to rotate out a spent bulb and replace it with a new one in no time. Chloe marveled at this bit of ingenuity.

They explored the rest of what the upstairs had to offer, including a video and displays about the lives of the many keepers who had lived there over the course of 75 years. "Which one do you think is the ghost?" Chloe asked.

"My money's on Elijah O'Connor," said George. "He was here the longest, and he has those haunted-looking eyes."

"I thought the same thing." She looked around one more time before they went back downstairs to formulate a plan to escape the island. The rain had slowed quite a bit, but still not enough to make the prospect of jumping back into the kayaks appealing.

"Let me pull up the radar," said George. He pulled out his phone, which was also wrapped in plastic. "It looks like the storm will be over in an hour at the latest."

"We have umbrellas here if you'd like to hike around the island while you wait," the docent said.

They accepted the umbrellas and stepped out into the rain. There was a dirt trail leading from the house that encircled the island. It meandered through the windblown cedars. The remainder of the maple leaves that had been clinging to their branches hours ago had fallen in the storm, and the trail was slick and coated with them. Even in the filtered sunlight, the red and yellow path they created glowed.

"I wish the weather was better, but I'm glad you agreed to come out. You and your family are just remarkable," said George.

"That's a kind way to put it."

"I'm serious. Your mom's speech was hilarious and your sister Betsy, well, I danced with her last night." He guided Chloe ahead of him, his hand on her lower back, as they came to a narrow section of the path.

"I saw that. It looked like she was teaching you some new moves, Mr. Dance Lessons."

He laughed. "She was. She seems to be self-taught."

"She is. She discovers the latest dance moves as soon as they've been invented while the rest of us up here don't know about them until they're already dated."

"It must be nice to live so close to her, your parents too."

"It is. Betsy and I live right down the street from each other. That can be both a blessing and a curse. You know how it is with siblings. We butt heads sometimes, but usually we get along pretty well."

"I do know how it is. Arthur and I used to be close. We've had a couple of fallings-out though."

"Oh?" Chloe barely knew Arthur, but she had

trouble imagining anyone having a quarrel with him.

"We two were the youngest kids, and he was so quiet and sensitive. I was more boisterous, more like his older brother than his twin. He resented my talents and successes as he got older."

Arthur hadn't seemed like the resentful type, but family dynamics were complicated. It was possible that he was jealous. George seemed to think very highly of himself, however, so maybe it was his arrogance that irked Arthur more than his triumphs. Chloe was more amused than annoyed by George, but she could imagine his shtick wearing thin after a while.

"My parents favored him and did things for him that they would never have done for me," George said. "When he bought the farm, they gave him a large sum of money to help with the down payment, never offering me a thing. I think they understood his endeavors better than mine. The world of farming is one that they're familiar with. I came to understand that and got what I wanted on my own."

"What was it that you wanted?"

"To make decisions. To make things happen for people. People like you, for instance."

"I can appreciate that. So many things feel out of our control. I can relate to the family issues too. Betsy is closer to my mom than I am. I used to take it personally, but I don't anymore. They have more in common with each other." Chloe was closer with her dad than her sisters were. Not close, he didn't let anyone in really close to him, but closer. It seemed like

George would've had a tight relationship with his dad as well. Roy was proud of him. That much was evident.

They strolled across a wooden bridge that spanned a babbling brook. Leaves bounced and jostled in the eddying water, and Chloe dropped in a twig, watching it float from one side to the other.

George crouched down next to her. "Giving him the money, being more protective of him, those things in themselves would've been fine," he said. "But then I moved back up to the area about three years ago so that I could be closer to everyone."

"You did? I don't remember seeing you."

"It didn't last long. I got involved with a woman that Arthur claimed he had been interested in. I'm still not sure if he developed the interest before or after I started dating her. He wouldn't speak to me, even after I broke it off with her, and it became so uncomfortable that I gave up on living here altogether. I left and haven't been around much since."

Was this true? It made Arthur sound petty, but there were always two sides to a story. The fact that George asked Arthur if he could dance with her last night lent some credence to it though. Maybe George had been trying to avoid another rift. Maybe Arthur wasn't so mellow after all.

Would he be upset that she had gone kayaking with his brother today? Arthur himself had claimed that he was only interested in friendship with her, so Chloe thought it would be fine but, if George's account was accurate, it was difficult to say for sure.

"Things must be better between you two now. You were out together the night of Hannah's bachelorette party," she said.

"We have an uneasy truce. I'm on edge now that I'm back, but I'm only staying long enough to see the project through. Once the property's established, I'll be on my way."

"You're doing a service to the community, you know. A lot of people, me included, were opposed to tearing down the library, but a couple of new local businesses and nice apartments will go a long way towards mending fences."

"Thanks," George said. "I love that you're interested in being involved."

Reaching an offshoot of the trail, they followed it to a sandy beach. Chloe sat down. The rain had ceased, but the gray sky persisted. George's hand brushed hers as he joined her, and he kept it there. She moved her hand safely into her lap.

George pulled a lighter from his pocket, flicking it. He watched the flame wobble before letting go and starting over again. Chloe hoped that he wasn't planning on smoking. She wasn't in the mood to smell like an ashtray on top of being wet and chilled.

"I don't smoke," he said. He must have noticed her giving him a sideways glare. "I used to, though. Playing with this thing's become a habit. I often don't even realize I'm doing it, like right now." He chuckled and stuck it back in his pocket. "I think it's stopped raining. Do you want to return the umbrellas?"

"Sure. I'm ready to head back," said Chloe. This

had been fun, but last night was catching up to her. She was tempted to take a nap here on the beach.

They walked back to the house, returned the umbrellas, and found their kayaks where they had left them. George held her hand as he helped her in and gave her that look, the one he had given her when they tangoed at the tavern. It was like he couldn't help himself, even when he was trying to keep it professional.

Their paddle back to shore took a quarter of the effort and half the time of their initial voyage. They sailed in, hopped out, and pulled the kayaks up to join the others.

Chloe surveyed the choppy expanse of Lake Michigan that she had just crossed, two times on a stormy October day no less, and felt like she really could tackle anything.

"We did it," George said. "See? We make a great team."

At these words, a spell was lifted. Was that what this adventure had been all about, convincing Chloe that they could work together? Making her feel invincible? Had there really been an investor who had cancelled their plans, or was that all part of the ruse?

If it was a trick, George had almost succeeded. Chloe had been so caught up with the thrill of surviving their paddle to the island that she had let her guard down. She had questioned him, just a little, about the legitimacy of what he was up to, but his simple reassurance had been enough. If she was being honest with herself, she had been ready to sign on the dotted line if that's what it took to get her precious shop.

It was still possible that this would all work out just fine, but she needed to be a lot more cautious around George in the future. If he knew what he was doing, he was astonishingly good at it.

Chapter Twelve

In Which Some Things are Rotten

Chloe rolled past the excavator in the library parking lot and stopped next to the curb. She couldn't believe the old building would really be gone forever after today. She had visited often as a child, usually tagging along with Hannah. They brought home piles of books. Still a non-fiction fanatic, Chloe read about everything from airplanes to space to deep sea creatures. The library had been a community gathering place for over one hundred years, starting its life as a general store and later becoming the Namur Public Library. It would be missed by many and she was sorry to see it go.

Stepping out of her truck, she heard yelling coming from the direction of the building. What's going on? She jogged closer to find out.

"What do we want?"

"Our library!"

"When do we want it?"

"Now!" Connie, the former head librarian, stood on the steps of the doomed library with a megaphone, rallying her fellow citizens to halt its demolition. Five others joined her, pumping their fists and waving signs.

"Connie, let's be reasonable," Roy called up to her.

"The time for being reasonable is over," Connie yelled. "We want our library."

"You have the mobile library," said Roy, pointing out the bookmobile, which was stationed at the far side of the lot.

Connie ignored him. "What do we want?"

"The excavator is running. We need you to clear out." Roy ducked under the caution tape to confront the protestors. "I don't want to have to get the police involved, but you're going to force my hand."

The crowd was not impressed by his threats. So much so, in fact, that one of them reached into a paper grocery bag and pulled out a rotten cabbage. Roy backed away with his hands out, ready to defend himself from an onslaught of vegetables. "The board has made its decision. You need to accept this."

"Never," said Connie. She raised her fist and the protestors cheered. Any trace of her usually proper demeanor had vanished in the wake of this imminent loss. Her crimson face coordinated with her tailored skirt suit. Errant pieces of hair stuck out of a usually perfect bun. She whipped off her stylish heels and threw them at Roy.

The other protestors cheered and a tomato was lobbed, narrowly missing Roy's head. He hiked up his overalls and postured himself in a wide stance, as if he wouldn't be intimidated by the rabble on the porch.

Chloe couldn't help but notice, though, that he had positioned himself well out of throwing range.

The construction foreman looked on, clearly at a loss. The driver of the excavator, however, was engrossed in a gardening catalogue and hadn't looked up at all. Maybe this kind of thing was more common than one would expect.

Chloe couldn't look away. Two strong personalities were facing off and the fireworks had just begun. She crossed the lot and joined Wes and Bea. They stood next to the bookmobile, watching the scene unfold. Wes leaned against it as if he was exhausted already. This was a difficult day for him, and he probably wanted to get it over with.

"I'm going up there," Wes said. He crossed the lot, ducked under the caution tape, and bounded up the steps. Laying his hand on her shoulder, he whispered something in Connie's ear. Whatever it was, it had an enormous effect. She crumpled, leaning her head against his chest. Her shoulders heaved. She was sobbing. He rubbed her back and guided her down the steps.

Chloe felt a tightness building around her temples. She had been prepared to feel a little guilty coming here, but she had wanted to show her support to Wes. Seeing how much the library meant to Connie and the other people on the steps of the library brought her a whole new level of discomfort. Could the library have been saved? Had Roy been clearing the way for his son, and by extension Chloe, when he advocated for its demolition, or had it truly been too far gone?

It really was a beautiful place, ornate in a way that newer buildings didn't even aspire to anymore. The roof of the front porch was supported with carved wooden columns. The thick front door, similarly adorned with leaves and flowers, was topped with a block announcing that it had been built in 1916. It was a shame that it hadn't been maintained, but it was too late for regrets.

Connie retrieved her shoes and slid them back on. Wes walked her to her car; she drove away. With the departure of their fearless leader, the other protestors lost steam. The guy with the bag of rotten vegetables took a parting shot at the excavator, splattering a rotten eggplant across its windshield. He had quite an arm. Chloe was impressed with his accuracy.

When the last of the protestors drove away and the eggplant was sufficiently removed, the construction foreman double-checked that the area was clear inside and out. He motioned the excavator forward. It rumbled towards the building, its great claw reaching down to dig into the roof.

Wes, who had returned, looked on sadly. Bea took his hand. "I guess that's that," he said. "They really went through with it. I hadn't realized how much I was betting on some kind of a miracle until now. This bookmobile had me believing in last minute second chances." He patted its side.

The bookmobile had been sitting in a garage for thirty years when, unbeknownst to Wes, his best friend Hugh and a group of mechanics in Madison set about restoring it. It had been in really rough shape, but now it looked just as it had when it first rolled into town in the 1950s.

"I think I've seen enough," said Wes. "I'm going to do my rounds now. Do either of you want to come along?" He opened the driver's side door of the bookmobile, ready to hop in.

"I'll ride along for a little while, but then I have to get back to the farm," said Bea.

Chloe declined altogether. She needed to meet with Drake at the bank to discuss her business plan, including the possibility of having a storefront. Telling her friends about it could wait until she knew more.

On the other hand, maybe there was a reason that she hadn't disclosed anything yet. The library had been so important to all of them, especially to Wes. It had been his safe haven growing up, during a time when he felt like an outsider nearly everywhere else. He would've done anything to have saved it. Would it be a slap in the face if Chloe set up a shop atop the ruins of his childhood sanctuary? When she put it that way, the answer was almost certainly yes.

Between questions about George's sincerity and her guilt about potentially profiting from the demolition of a structure that had been the heart of this community, Chloe had a lot to think about.

Wes and Bea climbed into the bookmobile and waved goodbye. Chloe went back to her truck to get her briefcase and walked down Main Street, heading for the bank. When she got there, the receptionist recognized her and asked her to take a seat.

"Mr. Grossman will be with you in a moment," she said.

Walking out from behind the desk, she entered a room with a frosted glass door. Chloe heard the mumble of the receptionist's voice followed by Drake's attempt at a whisper. "Make her wait for a while longer. It's a power move."

The receptionist came back out and said, "He's on the phone with a very important client. It'll just be a little bit longer."

Chloe nodded in approval. "Power move."

The young woman blushed and scooted back to her seat. Chloe looked around. Why did banks always try to make their waiting areas look like somebody's living room? They had a fireplace with pictures of their associates on the mantel and a little plaque that said "Love Grows Here". It's like they wanted her to think that they all lived here as one happy family. Maybe Drake would come out in a robe and slippers, puffing on a pipe. Now that would be a power move.

Chloe tried not to chuckle to herself. She spent a lot of time trying not to laugh at her notions in public. It kept her spirits up. Did other people do that? Arthur seemed to amuse himself a lot. She admired that about him.

The phone rang at the front desk and the receptionist answered. "Yes. Excellent. Thank you, sir." She hung up. "Mr. Grossman is available to see you now."

Chloe stood and headed into his office. When

she opened the door he was on the phone, and he held up a finger to let her know that he would be with her in a moment. "Yes, Mr. Mayor. It's my pleasure. Always happy to be of service." How had he found time to get on the phone with the mayor? Wasn't he just talking to the receptionist? "That's too sweet. Tell your wife I'll see her at your Halloween party tomorrow night." He hung up and chuckled, shaking his head. "Sorry about that. I'm so in demand lately. You know how it is." Chloe sat down and made a valiant attempt to keep a straight face.

"So, you're thinking about renting a storefront and you've come to me to see what I can do for you." He leaned back, crossing his arms behind his head. His tie peeked out from the bottom of his jacket, where his button was unfastened. Why did he refuse to fasten that bottom button?

Chloe tried to ignore it, but it was a struggle. "Yes. I have my business proposal here. I'm wondering if the bank could offer me a loan." She slid her paperwork, which she had been poring over all week, across the desk towards him.

"Let's take a looksie," he said.

He scanned through the papers, humming and hawing. He pursed his lips and shook his head. "I don't know. The issue here is that your revenue is very inconsistent. You need to be secure in knowing that you'll be able to afford your rent every month. And then there's the insurance and point of sale issues, inventory, marketing...You're going to need a very large loan upfront. You may represent too much of a risk for us right now."

Chloe understood where he was coming from. She had been surprised by the costs of getting started as well.

"But..." he continued, leaning across the desk towards her. "We may be able to continue this discussion over dinner. What are you doing tomorrow night?"

Ha! She had plans. "I can't tomorrow. I'm going to be at Lindsay's Halloween party."

"Well then, I might just have to make an appearance there." He smiled at her in a way that she assumed was meant to be winning but only succeeded in making him look pained.

"Tomorrow night? That's Halloween. Don't you have a party at the mayor's tomorrow night?" What mayor had he been pretending to talk to? They didn't even have a mayor.

His face fell, but he recovered quickly. "Yes. That's right. I do have another, very exclusive, party to attend. Well then, what about next Saturday?"

Shoot, she wasn't doing anything next Saturday. That Drake. She could see through him so clearly he was like a window that had just been wiped down with vinegar. If she didn't agree to go out with him, this was the end of the road for her aspirations to have a shop. It had been a long-shot, and this was the only bank where they knew her personally. It was probably the only place where she wouldn't be laughed out the door.

"I'm free next Saturday," she heard herself saying. What was she thinking?

"Excellent," Drake said, leaning back again. This was madness. She had to endure George and now this? It was further proof that the only men who were interested in her were either creeps or had some kind of ulterior motive. Fine, if this was how it was going to go, two could play at this game. She'd do what it took to get ahead.

"Pick you up next Saturday then?" he asked. "Six o'clock. My treat." He pushed the paperwork back to her and she felt her skin crawl.

"That's the copy I prepared for you," she said. "You should keep it."

"You can feel free to hang onto it for now. There will be plenty of time to talk about your options over dinner."

Chapter 13

In Which a Chapter's Unlucky Number Lives Up to its Reputation

Chloe bumped along in Arthur's truck. It wasn't as ancient as Old Blue, but it was close. She'd have to introduce the two of them sometime.

Dirty water sprayed the windows, slowly coating them with a brown film of mud. She wasn't sure if it was wise to go any farther, but the set look on Arthur's face said that he was going full speed ahead. Nothing was going to keep him from his favorite hunting spot.

"You know," she said, "I once heard about a puddle on a road like this that was eight feet deep, at least. It looked shallow and wide so people kept driving right into it and getting irretrievably stuck."

"If they were irretrievably stuck, wouldn't there have been a bunch of trucks in the hole? How big was it?"

"Big enough."

"Pshaw."

"Did you just say 'pshaw'?"

"I did."

"Care to elaborate?"

"Gladly. In order for the puddle to accommodate multiple trucks, it would have to be gigantic."

"Not necessarily..."

"Besides, once one fell in, the others should've been able to see that it wasn't safe to drive into."

"Well, they all got out eventually. Let's not get hung up on the specifics," she said. Arthur shot her his grin, which she now thought of as amused in a sweet way. "The point is, it's possible."

"If you say so."

"I do. I have it on good authority that it's a true story." She had exaggerated about the depth of the puddle a bit, and the trucks had all been pulled out, but that truly did happen. She remembered it well, because her dad had to repair the water damaged vehicles afterwards. He gave a speech at dinner every night for a month about not driving through standing water, and Chloe had never forgotten it.

The memory was particularly vivid right now. She cringed every time they approached another puddle. She tried avoiding watching the road, which could more accurately be called a trail at this point, by looking out the window at the woods. She could see a great distance and there was no end in sight. She was grateful that they had cell phones, because it would be a long walk home if they got stuck and couldn't call anyone.

"I've been down this road hundreds of times in much worse conditions. There's no way...No way..." Arthur had been driving slowly and steadily, but now they were at a standstill. He pressed down on the accelerator and the tires spun and whirred. Clods of mud smacked the windows. They were stuck.

"Just a minute," he said. "It'll be fine. We're not stuck." They were so stuck. Chloe knew it and she knew that he knew it. He wasn't going to admit it now though, not after he had just said there was no way it could happen.

"Alright," he said. "I'm going to need you to slide over into the driver's seat."

"Now?" she asked. He was still sitting there. She was tempted but...

"I'm going to get out and push while you gradually press on the gas."

"Thanks for clarifying."

"What do you mean?"

"Nothing. I don't mean anything at all. Sounds like a plan." That could've been awkward.

"I'll raise my hand for you to start, and then do it again when I want you to stop." She nodded and waited for him to climb out before sliding over.

She looked in the rearview mirror, barely able to see him in the red glow of the tail lights, and waited for his signal. When he raised his hand, she pressed on the gas. She looked back again and stopped. Arthur was splattered with mud from head to foot.

He clumped over to her side of the truck, wiping mud from his face. If they ever made it out hunting he would be very effectively camouflaged.

"Why did you stop?" he asked.

"Because I'm spraying you with mud."

"I'm fine. I can't get any muddier than I already am, so don't worry about it. Just go for it." He strode back to try again. She pressed down on the accelerator, harder this time, but all she accomplished was spraying Arthur once more. It turned out that he could get muddier.

"This isn't working," he said, returning to state the obvious. "We're really close to my tree stand though, so I propose that we walk over there and hunt for a while, if that's ok with you."

"That's great with me. I thought our day might've been shot." She chuckled.

"Was that a pun?"

"It was, sorry. I'm pretty terrible."

He smiled. "I've heard worse."

"I've said worse."

"We've probably scared away every deer for miles, but we can still sit there for an hour or two, just until it's late enough to call someone. Tom lives close by. He'll be able to come over with his tractor and pull us out. I'd call him now, but I'd hate to wake him up this early."

"Sounds like a plan." Chloe hopped out of the truck and handed him a towel. He wiped off the larger clumps of dirt. He was left with a thin coating all over his face and hands and his clothes were caked.

"Are you sure you're going to be alright out here?" Chloe asked. It was a chilly morning. He looked like he would be freezing in minutes.

"I'm fine," he said. "Today is balmy relative to what it'll be like in January. This'll toughen me up."

He reached into the truck for his bow case, and they tromped over thick leaves and rotten logs to get to the tree stand. It was rough going, but Chloe kept up. When they reached a fallen tree, he took her hand and held on for a while as they walked farther into the forest. Resisting George's charms had been easy, as obvious and silly as he was. Arthur was a different story; he was so sweet and sincere.

There was no doubt that he was one of a kind, but it was difficult to believe that he just wanted to have a friendly sit in the woods alone with her. Who did that? Certainly no one she knew. It was possible, she supposed, just unusual. Maybe she wanted to believe that he might be interested in something more. How had he gotten under her skin so quickly and seemingly without effort?

When they reached the tree stand, Arthur helped her get strapped into the harness that would keep her from falling out. He tightened it around her waist, leaving a dirt streak on her hip. He tried to brush it off then realized what he was doing and stepped back, blushing. "Sorry," he said.

"It's all in the name of safety," Chloe replied. He stepped into his own harness and showed her how to climb. It was quite easy. They were soon perched side by side on the suspended metal platform. "Are we allowed to talk?" she asked.

"Yes. But you have to whisper really quietly."

"How long do you usually have to wait for the deer to come along?"

"It's up to the deer. Sometimes five minutes,

sometimes they don't show up at all."

"That would be rude. We've come gone to great lengths to get here."

"I agree, but try telling that to the deer."

They sat there quietly for a while. Chloe usually felt uncomfortable with silence, but she noted once again that there was something about Arthur that made her feel at ease. She started feeling drowsy. Her head nodded, and she snapped back to attention. The second time she started to nod, she fell asleep.

She woke up groggily, smacking her lips. Feeling something warm and soft against her cheek, she snuggled in. The blanket smelled familiar, like pine needles and cologne. She bolted upright, suddenly remembering where she was and who she was with. That wasn't a blanket. It was Arthur's muddy jacket. She had fallen asleep on his shoulder. And was that drool? How embarrassing.

"It's a good thing you're strapped in, or I might've lost you," he teased.

"I can't believe I did that. Sorry about your jacket." She wiped his shoulder.

"It's fine. I don't mind at all. I fall asleep up here all the time."

"Really?"

"Yes, really. It's relaxing."

"How long was I asleep?"

"Half an hour or so. Do you want to stay up here a little longer?"

"Sure, just a little." Now that she was awake again, she admired the view. Most of the trees were bare and early morning sunlight hit the forest floor, illuminating bright orange mushrooms sprouting from a dead standing tree. A cedar waxwing called out from an oak. A bird in the distance called back with an identical melody.

She heard one crunch and then another, as if someone was stepping carefully through the leaves just beyond their sight. Arthur put his hand on her arm, signaling her to be quiet and still. A deer emerged from behind a tangle of shrubs. The doe was elegant, with a long neck and dainty legs, her chestnut body sleek and smooth. She browsed around in the open woods for a while. Lifting her nose to the air, she sniffed, pulling back her lips. She snorted and turned back in the direction that she had come, disappearing into the underbrush.

"That was incredible," Chloe whispered, grabbing Arthur's arm. He looked down at her hand. It looked like he wanted to say something. Instead, he looked away.

"It never gets old either." He scanned the trees, avoiding looking over at her.

"Do you think she smelled us?"

"She could have. Deer are wary this time of year, and they have an excellent sense of smell."

"Do you think we'll see any more?" she asked.

"We could. Once you see a doe, the bucks are usually not too far behind."

They sat there for a while longer, until Arthur thought that it was late enough to call Tom, who picked up on the first ring. When they hung up, Arthur said, "He said he's been up for hours and will be right over. He knew just the spot I was talking about, too. Apparently it's a common place to get stuck."

Chloe didn't want to say I told you so, but she was tempted, especially because he didn't believe her puddle story.

"It'll take him a while to get here. We can stay in the tree for a bit, if you'd like to," Arthur said.

"Let's stay." She was enjoying the view and the company. They sat next to each other, looking out into the forest and listening for more crunching leaves. Chloe felt the weight of whatever he had left unsaid hanging between them, and she wished she could read Arthur as easily as she could Bea. The same inscrutability that made him intriguing was threatening to drive her crazy.

Why was she afraid to address the elephant in the tree stand? They were clearly attracted to each other, and she had never been shy about saying something before. This felt different though, somehow. It felt too important. Maybe it would be best to go against her instincts on this one, if she wanted it to go differently than it usually did. And she did want it to go differently. She wanted it to go better, if it went anywhere at all.

"Are you ready to go?" Arthur asked. "I think I can hear Tom coming." Chloe listened. She could hear the rumble of a tractor as well. They climbed down and he offered to help her step out of her harness.

"I think I can manage," she said, almost falling over. He supported her by the elbow to help her stabilize and squeezed it twice before letting go. See? She wasn't imagining things.

Tom was just pulling in when they got to the truck. "How'd you manage this one?" Tom asked, laughing. He looked Arthur up and down, taking in his mud streaked clothes and face. "Wait 'til I tell the fellas at Emma's. You're the third person I've had to rescue this month. I should erect a sign here with my phone number."

"I really thought I could make it. How many times have I been back here? But Chloe here had to go ahead and tell me a story about people getting stuck in a giant puddle."

"So this is my fault?" she said. They were all laughing now. Tom had no trouble pulling the truck free from the mud. The two hunters thanked Tom, hopped into the liberated truck, and drove backwards for a while until they could turn around.

"I'm glad you were here when I got stuck," Arthur said. "It's easier to maintain a sense of humor when you have an audience."

"I'm glad I was here too. Now I just have to go home and get ready for the Halloween party tonight. Are you still going?"

"I wouldn't miss it for the world," he said, pulling onto a proper road. "Are you dressing up?"

"Of course. I found a gorgeous banana costume that fits me like a glove." It was massive and warm and she adored it. "What's your costume?"

"I'm going to keep you in suspense until tonight."

"You don't know what you're wearing yet, do you?

"Not a clue."

"You're kind of a man of mystery, did you know that?"

"Me? Not at all. I'm pretty straightforward."

"You think so?"

"Sure. I usually try to be transparent. Why, is there something you're dying to know?" There was that grin again.

Yes, there was, as a matter of fact. But she wasn't going to be the one to say it. "Nothing specific. I just have a hunch that there's more to you than meets the eye."

"That's funny, because I was thinking the same thing about you," he said.

"Me? No way. I'm not afraid to speak my mind."

He shrugged. "I guess we'll just have to wait and see."

"Yes," she said. "I guess we will."

Chapter Fourteen

In Which Surprises Prove to be a Mixed Lot

"You came early," said Lindsay. She took the stack of pumpkin brownies from Chloe's arms and set them on a long table that was already laden with snacks, desserts, and drinks. "You are a lifesaver. Seriously. This month would've been a disaster without you. And you're a giant banana. I love it. Did you bring Betsy along too?"

Chloe twirled. With her blonde hair and a bit of yellow face paint, she made the ideal banana. "Betsy ran inside right away when we got here. She and Grace are putting the finishing touches on their makeup. Where's your costume?"

"I'm French toast. Grace sewed it for me and it turned out really cute. I'll get dressed after I'm finished setting up."

"Ooh. I can't wait to see it. We can be breakfast together. Look at all these decorations." The chandelier was draped in cobwebs, jack-o-lanterns grinned out from every nook and cranny, and life sized creepy statues were stationed at doorways. The round tables were draped in gauzy black fabric topped with ornate candelabras. "How did you do it? I can't believe

Hannah's wedding was here less than a week ago. This place is completely transformed again."

"Grace did most of the decorating. She's really crafty and a massive Halloween fan, so it came naturally to her," said Lindsay.

Bea and Wes came in carrying even more plates of food, including Bea's famous Belgian pies. They were dressed as Cleopatra and Mark Antony. Wes looked a bit glum. "Sorry for the long face guys. I'll liven up as the night goes on. I'm still recovering from seeing the library being torn down."

"I'm so sorry," said Lindsay. "You did all you could."

Wes nodded. "It was my favorite place growing up here. It was also the reason I came back. I have a lot to thank it for." He hugged Bea. They wouldn't have reconnected if he hadn't come back to try to save it.

"Your costumes are great," said Chloe.

"Thanks," Bea twirled. "Wes came up with them. I think I scared my goats tonight though." She picked a piece of straw out of her wig. "How many people are you expecting?"

"I'm not sure," said Lindsay. "We sold about 100 tickets online, but people can buy them at the door too."

"Wow. It's a hit. This might become a tradition," Chloe said.

Lindsay agreed. "They're going to start arriving any time. Do you guys mind manning the door while I get dressed?"

"I can do it. I've never been a bouncer before." Wes widened his stance to look more impressive. He and Bea walked over to the door while Chloe unwrapped plates of food at the table. She stole a brownie and munched on it while looking around to see if there was anything else to be done. Everything seemed to be in order. She poured herself some green punch and sat down at a table. True to her word, Lindsay had procured her own straw bale seats for the event.

Moments later, Betsy and Grace bolted in dressed as witches. Sexy witches, naturally. They ran over to Chloe's table and sat down.

"Do you know if George is coming tonight?" Betsy asked.

"No. I'm not sure." She emphasized that she didn't care either by taking another bite of brownie.

"I hope he does," Betsy said. "He is the most interesting thing to happen around here since...well, ever."

"He's trouble. You have to be able to see that."

Now it was Betsy's turn to shrug. "I like trouble."

Chloe let it go. She knew that she would drive Betsy straight to him if she tried to warn her away any further. "Do what you like."

"I always do." Didn't Chloe know it.

At the door, costumed people started to trickle in. So many of them wore masks that it was difficult to know who was who. A tall person, probably a man, arrived wearing a full gorilla suit. Maybe she'd take a picture with him later. A gorilla and a banana...Chloe chuckled to herself.

The DJ, who had been setting up on stage, played The Monster Mash, and a group of zombies took to the floor. Chloe was about to get up and join them when Arthur walked in. When she had played it over in her mind before the party, she waited for him to approach her. She would be chatting with a circle of friends, and everyone would be laughing at a witty comment she had just made when he would step up next to her. "Oh, hello," she would say, as if she had just noticed him.

In reality, it was difficult to resist striding across the room. He pulled down on the sleeves of a red velvet jacket with gold buttons; it looked a bit snug. He wore tall leather boots. A foam parrot perched on his shoulder, and he held a hook in his hand. George followed behind him, dressed as a slim King Henry the Eighth.

Betsy had no restraint. She ran up to George and wrapped her arms around his neck, kissing him on the cheek like she did with everyone. They all took it as a personal compliment, and George was no exception. His usual expression of boredom mixed with arrogance shifted to pleasant surprise. She pulled him out onto the dance floor. He didn't object at all to the attention and joined her in another one of her wild dances.

Chloe didn't realize that Arthur was sitting down next to her until he cleared his throat. "Your costume is very fitting," he said.

"You think of me as a giant banana sort of person?"

"Hmm...yes. I think so."

"For some reason I just had to go for it this year. Look at you though. You and George look like you stepped off a film set. The Tudors of the Caribbean..." She was cracking herself up again.

"George has a whole trunk full of costumes." He rubbed his neck and looked away. He must have been cajoled into dressing up.

"You look very dashing. Cleaner than you were the last time I saw you, too."

"Why thank you. The mud washed right off. Can I get you another drink?"

"That would be lovely." She handed him her cup, and he headed to the punch bowl. A slow song started and Chloe amused herself by admiring the pairings out on the dance floor. A crayon danced with a gumball machine. A hot dog was paired up with a unicorn. A certain witch was looking very cozy with King Henry the Eighth. Chloe wondered where the gorilla had gone. She scanned the room but didn't spot him.

Arthur returned with a drink in each hand, one for himself and one for Chloe. "Thanks. I needed this," Chloe said, "I'm getting pretty warm. Would you like to take another walk through the orchard?"

"I would love that. If I'm hot in this get-up, you must be sweltering."

She took his arm, and they walked out the door. The roar of the party faded as it closed behind them. The orchard was dark, lit only by the flashing lights streaming through the windows. A bat swooped above their heads before disappearing into the night.

"Whoa," said Chloe, "a Halloween bat. That's creepy. I've never seen them out this late in the year before."

"Me either. I wonder what he's up to."

"Maybe she's a vampire."

"That's the most likely explanation."

"Some people think I'm a vampire."

"Oh really?"

"Yes. Except they only see me during the day, never at night." She tried to look mysterious, but it was difficult to pull off while covered in yellow face paint.

"I don't know if I should be walking alone with you then," said Arthur. "Although you've made an exception and come out at night, so maybe your powers have weakened."

"No way, my powers never weaken."

"I believe that. Hey, let me know if you ever want to go hunting with me again. I can't promise that there will always be that much excitement but...."

"I think we could find ways to keep it interesting." Oops. That had sneaked out unexpectedly. She checked his reaction. He either hadn't heard her or had chosen not to respond.

This costume was making her feel mischievous. It provided an escape route. She could say anything and then tuck her arms, legs, and head in and hide from the consequences for a while. Nothing to see here, just a giant banana. "I mean, it was fun. I'd love to go again."

When it got so dark that it was difficult to see in front of them, she sat down and patted the ground next to her. Arthur joined her, leaning back on his elbows and looking up at the moon through the thin branches of a cherry tree. An owl hooted in the distant forest beyond the orchard.

"Did you hear that?" he said. "First a bat and now an owl, nature is really getting into the spirit tonight. Halloween was my favorite holiday as a kid."

"It was?" Chloe thought that Christmas was kind of a given for most people.

"Sure. I was kind of timid. I guess I liked to think of myself as the strong and silent type. On Halloween I could dress up as anything, be anyone I wanted to be. I was usually a superhero of some kind or another. The candy probably gave it a solid nudge into the favorite category as well."

"Oh yes. The candy was a big draw for us. My sisters and I would dump all of it out on the living room floor at the end of the night and sort it into categories. We traded each other for our favorites. Betsy drove a hard bargain, but Hannah would trade me for anything. She always ended up with the peanut butter toffees."

"We did the same thing. Guess who the shrewd businessman was at our house."

"Hmm...let me guess..." They both laughed and turned to look at each other.

Arthur stopped laughing but maintained his

little grin. "You said something about keeping it interesting..." So he had heard her. "I'd like to kiss you, if that's alright."

"Then why don't you?"

He sat up and cupped her face in his hands. Judging from the intensity of his gaze, he had been thinking about doing this all day as well. So he did want to kiss her. She had known it all along.

Now that they were finally here, she could tell that he wanted to take his time. She could wait. The corners of her mouth turned up in a smile and he leaned forward, pressing his lips into hers. Leaning closer, she suppressed a sigh. His lips were soft and sweet and she wanted to stay there longer but he pulled away, standing up and taking her hand.

"Maybe we should be getting back," he said.

"Maybe we shouldn't." She spun to face him. He tried to pull her close, but her banana poked him in the thigh. "Well, it was fun while it lasted." Chloe pretended to walk away. "Just kidding." She flung the banana over her head and into the grass. Wrapping her arms around his neck, she skirted around the parrot and kissed him again with more urgency this time.

Kissing Arthur wasn't anything like she had expected it to be, it was so much better. He was so delicious that she was tempted to actually bite him, vampire-style. She already had the reputation; she might as well live up to it. She lightly nipped his neck. He didn't seem to mind at all. He grinned at her in a slightly different way than he usually did, and Chloe felt her knees nearly give way beneath her.

"Do you still want to go back?" she asked.

He leaned in close, ready to kiss her again. "Not particularly."

"I don't either, but you had a point."

"I disagree with myself now though."

"Me too, but I'm afraid if we're gone too long, Lindsay will send out a search party. I don't want to be caught with my peel down. That's the most embarrassing thing that can happen to a banana."

"When you put it that way…"

"Don't worry; it's just a rain check."

When she had reluctantly reinstated her peel, she kissed him one last time, in awkward banana costume fashion. It was worth the effort. They walked back through the orchard arm in arm. She could feel Arthur looking at her and then glancing away, and she tried to keep her face in the shadows for fear that he would see the matching silly smile on her own face. When they emerged into the light near the barn again, she turned towards him and gazed into his eyes.

"Arthur?"

"Yes?"

"Your face is covered in yellow paint." He felt his face and looked at his fingers. They came away yellow.

He ran away, ducking inside, presumably to wash up in the bathroom. She felt a warm glow spreading through her chest. Arthur was wonderful and perfect and sweet and talented and…there was the gorilla, waiting in line to use the porta potty that Lindsay had to rent because of the large crowd. Chloe wouldn't approach him for a picture now, that would be weird, but she'd ask him when he passed this way on his walk back.

Right before stepping in, he took off his mask, fanned his face, and slid it back on. It all happened in an instant, but it was long enough for Chloe to see who was hiding under there. It was Steve.

What was he doing here? There was no way that Lindsay had invited her ex or was aware of his presence. Was he spying on her? This was ridiculous. If he wanted to keep pulling this nonsense, Chloe was going to match him with some nonsense of her own. Ridiculous times called for ridiculous measures.

She looked around. No one else was outside. There was a rope coiled in the long grass at the edge of the yard. She sprinted to pick it up and wrapped it around and around the porta potty before tying it in a knot. One of the zombies stepped out of the barn, heading her way. What should she do?

"It's out of order," Chloe said. "You really do not want to go in there. I'm making sure no one uses it." The zombie looked at her with suspicion but walked back into the barn anyway.

Arthur passed the zombie on the way back out. Steve tried to open the door and, finding it locked, started pounded on it. "Hey, what's going on out there?" he yelled.

"Just a second," Chloe said in a squeaky voice that she hoped masked her real one. "There's something wrong with one of the hinges. If you open it, it'll break. I'm just fixing it."

"Is this a joke? Let me out of here."

"What are you doing?" Arthur asked.

She put a finger to her lips and shushed him. She whispered into his ear even more quietly than she had in the deer stand. "Lindsay's horrible husband is in there. He sneaked into the party in a gorilla costume."

Arthur's eyes widened. "So you trapped him in a porta potty?"

"What was I supposed to do? Lindsay can't know he's here, and he might not leave without a fuss."

"I don't know what you were supposed to do. Not that."

"Do you have a better suggestion?"

"No. I don't, but that doesn't mean this is a bright idea. What now? People are going to notice that you've got someone in there."

"We need to get rid of him," she said

"Excuse me?"

"Get your truck. We'll drag it down the road with him inside, just for a mile or two. If we leave it on the side of the county highway someone will find him and let him out. No harm done."

"No harm done?" Arthur looked dubiously at the roped-up porta potty.

"Please. He's truly awful. You have no idea."

"I'm breaking down this door," Steve yelled. He slammed against it, and the porta potty tipped precariously. He must have wisely reconsidered his escape plan. The banging stopped, but he continued to yell.

"Alright, I'll help you," said Arthur. "But I'm on record saying that this is a horrible idea."

"That's fine. If it makes you feel better about it."

Arthur ran to his truck and backed it up to the porta potty. He grabbed a chain and attached the toilet to the trailer hitch. They jumped in the truck and crawled down the road.

Chloe looked back. Their cargo was skidding along evenly behind them. Her heart was racing. As long as it didn't tip over or slide into the ditch, everything would be fine. This was not a well thought through plan, but she had been given very little time to orchestrate it. Besides, she was sick of Steve. If this didn't send that message loud and clear, she didn't know what would.

They didn't pass anyone along the way, and Chloe directed Arthur to a perfect spot. He unhooked Steve's temporary enclosure. Chloe hopped out. To say that her captive was furious would be a gross understatement, but sufficed to say that his wrathful oaths were shocking, even to a woman who had grown up in an auto repair shop.

Chloe yelled, "Leave Lindsay alone!" It didn't match the intensity of the vitriol coming from the porta potty but, once again, she hadn't been given much time. They both ran back into the truck and Arthur drove away, not looking back.

"That was the worst thing I ever did," he said, staring straight ahead like he had just seen something horrible.

"Or maybe it's the best thing you ever did."

"It would be really sad if that was the best thing I ever did."

"Second best."

"No, not even close."

Well, now that the toilet was safely in place, Chloe for one felt at peace with her rash decision. Lindsay would wonder where the porta potty went, but they could return it later, when Steve had escaped or been let out. He'd be freed in no time, so embarrassed that he'd never dare to show his face around here again.

"Now that we've left a guy alone in a porta potty on Halloween night, I'm going to need to know what's so awful about him," said Arthur. "I didn't know Steve very well, but from what I did know he seemed alright. Nowhere near bad enough to deserve that."

"The fact that he seemed alright is part of what makes it all so terrible. I still don't understand how he had everyone fooled." She filled him in on the nefarious adventures of the man formerly known as Lindsay's husband.

"I'm still a little horrified that I went along with that, but I can see where you're coming from. Besides, what was he doing at the party? Showing up in a gorilla costume to spy on the wife you just left is pretty unbalanced."

"Thank you, exactly. I'm going to drive past him on my way home to make sure he got out alright."

"I'll help you return it if no one is around."

"Thank you. You're my accomplice."

"Don't call me that."

When they got back to the party, they resumed their places at the table as if nothing had happened. Bea and Wes were already there. "What were you two up to?" Bea asked. "We had to start the games without you." Chloe loved games, but missing them had been worth it.

"Oh, we just took a stroll through the orchard," she replied. Bea gave her a look like she thought she knew what had really happened, but she didn't know half of it.

Lindsay joined them. She looked perplexed. "I know this is going to sound really bizarre, but does anyone know where my porta potty went?"

"That does sound bizarre," said Chloe. "Maybe a ghost took it."

"Maybe a ghost took it," Lindsay repeated. "Why does that make me think that you took it?" Chloe gasped at how offended she was at the mere suggestion that it could have been her. "I'm sorry," her suspicious friend said, "but it does seem like something you would do."

"The old me, maybe. The new me doesn't do things like that."

"Could the old you have taken over your body and done something like that while the new you was distracted? Does anyone else know anything about this?" Lindsay looked around the table for support. Everyone else had vanished.

"I guess lots of things are going missing tonight." Chloe said, prompting Lindsay to look at her like she was tempted to strangle her. "Ok. I'm going to be honest with you. I took the porta potty."

"I knew it!"

"But I can't tell you why." Lindsay started to object, but Chloe continued. "I need you to trust me on this one. It was for a good cause. I wouldn't have done it if it wasn't absolutely necessary. You'll have it back by tomorrow morning at the very latest. I promise."

"This is really strange, you know."

"I do know. I wasn't planning on it, I assure you."

"Fine. I'll trust you. But you need to explain eventually."

"I will. Just not tonight. It's better this way."

"If there's one thing I can say about this night, it's that it's been full of surprises," said Lindsay.

"Mostly good surprises."

"I agree. Mostly good ones."

Chapter Fifteen

Local Gorilla Has Halloween Fright
THE NAMUR PULSE
November 1, 20—
BY CATHERINE DUBOIX, Investigative Reporter

An unidentified individual was the victim of a cruel hoax yesterday evening. Although the exact details are unclear, it appears that a man wearing a gorilla costume entered a portable toilet at an unspecified location when an unknown person or persons sealed it with rope, trapping him inside. The toilet was then dragged down the road behind a vehicle. It was abandoned around 10:30pm in front of the home of a local reporter who, using her keen wits and unflinching sense of duty, released the man before notifying police. When the officer on duty, David Anselme, arrived at the scene, the gorilla had fled on foot and could not be located for questioning. Officer Anselme states that he has reason to believe that the gorilla was a specific target, and that this is an isolated incident. "Residents should not expect a rash of similar pranks in the following weeks," he said.

The gorilla was unavailable for comment.

Chapter Sixteen

In Which the Demeter Society
Makes its World Debut

Two days after the Halloween party, a documentary about the Demeter Society aired on public television. *Your Town* featured small towns across America with interesting food cultures and traditions. The film crew had arrived in Door County in late summer and filmed all four women at work. They also toured the town and highlighted its Walloon Belgian heritage.

There had been some debate about whether the women should limit their viewing party to the four members only, or if family should be invited as well. Not surprisingly, Bea and Sarah came down on the side of including family. Chloe and Lindsay voted to keep it to their small group, plus Bea's mom.

In the end, Chloe and Lindsay won out after Chloe painted a picture of certain members of her own family talking over the entire one hour show. (She didn't mention Roy, but he figured prominently into the equation as well.)

Sarah suggested that they could have a party afterwards at her house to celebrate with everyone else. The other women agreed that it struck just the right balance. Chloe envisioned their respective families, getting ready to watch it together. Her mom and Roy would make quite a pair, as would George and Betsy. Having everyone together would've been almost worth it just to hear the conversations and watch the antics unfold, but not worth enough to give up being able to enjoy the debut in peace.

Chloe was hosting the smaller gathering of the society beforehand. Lindsay would be arriving any minute. There was no mystery behind her request for a pre-show discussion. She had certainly seen the newspaper article and put two and two together.

When Lindsay got to the door, Chloe opened it cautiously and peeked out. "Hi?"

"Hi. I'm not mad at you. Let me in."

"You're not?" She opened it farther and Lindsay strode past her into the living room. They stood facing each other while Chloe picked some invisible lint off of her sweater.

"I don't think I need to ask who it was in that gorilla suit," said Lindsay.

"Probably not."

"How did this come about? How did you discover it was him?"

"Do you really want to know?"

"I'm not sure. It's one of those cases where

the less I know the better, but I'm too curious."

"You didn't know anything about it before-hand. It was all me."

"That's very true, but I would appreciate a basic recounting of the facts. Not knowing what happened is making it worse."

"Unfortunately, knowing what happened doesn't make it a whole lot better. I go from feeling like I did what I had to do to being sure that I've lost my mind. I'll tell you the basic story, and you can judge for yourself." Lindsay nodded. She still hadn't moved to sit down. "There I was, standing outside. I didn't have a care in the world. I was minding my own business. Little did I know that everything was about to change. I was going to have to make a choice…"

"Will you please get to the part where you figured out that it was Steve?"

"I'm getting to it. So there I was…" Lindsay groaned. Chloe was notorious for dragging out stories once she had an audience. "I'd noticed the gorilla earlier that evening, when he walked into the barn. He stood out because I was a banana." Chloe couldn't help but snicker.

"Seriously, Chloe?"

"Sorry." She composed herself. "But then I didn't see him for a while after that. I'm not sure what he was doing between his arrival and when he was in line at the bathroom."

"I don't remember seeing anyone like that at all," said Lindsay, wrapping her arms around herself.

"I would never have known that it was him, but he took off his mask for a second before he went into the bathroom. I think you can guess what happened next."

"I think I can too. That's all I wanted to know."

"What are you going to do now?" Chloe asked.

"I'm not sure. I've tried calling him, but he's never answered; I don't expect him to start now. I have a bad feeling about this. What if he's been watching me all along, and he just got caught this time?"

Lindsay finally sat down on the edge of the couch. Her back was ramrod straight, like she couldn't be comfortable until she saw the situation more clearly. Chloe joined her. She wanted to present a brilliant solution, wrapping everything up neatly and tying it off with a big bow. Even if there was such a solution though, she didn't have it. "I hope I didn't make things worse for you."

"I don't think you did. If anything, it sent the message loud and clear that people are looking out for me."

"And here I was, trying to be subtle," said Chloe. Some of the ridges that had been forming in Lindsay's brow smoothed out.

"Let's talk about something else, like what you were doing outside in the first place. By all accounts, you were gone for quite a while with a certain farmer."

"I'll tell you everything after you tell me about your dance with Harvey."

"That was nothing," said Lindsay. "We danced together for one song. He's been helping out at the bed and breakfast."

"I bet he has."

Lindsay look scandalized. "The very last thing I need is another man in my life."

"I know. I'm teasing…I bet it was fun though."

"It was. I have to admit it was nice to pretend that I had a normal, unencumbered life for an evening. Thanks for not telling me about…well…"

"Any time."

"How about just this time? We don't need to turn this into a habit or my events will develop a very unusual reputation." Another knock on the door interrupted their laughter.

"Come in," Chloe called. The other women bustled inside, simmering with anticipation. "Have a seat. I'll get everything started up and grab the snacks."

"I don't know if I can stand it," said Bea as she launched onto the couch, hugging her knees to her chest. Everyone got comfortable and Chloe went into the kitchen to grab the appetizers. Sarah followed behind her moments later to ask if she could help with anything.

"That would be great, thanks," said Chloe. She handed Sarah a cheese board.

"Arthur mentioned that he's been spending

some time with you," said Sarah.

"We have. I've discovered that I enjoy hunting. He's going to take me out again soon."

"I'm so pleased to hear that. He could use a friend. I worried that he was a becoming a bit closed off after his disappointment a few years back."

"Disappointment?"

"Oh. I'm so sorry...I shouldn't have said anything. I just assumed everyone knew."

"No. I hadn't heard anything about that at all."

"This is a bit awkward, but I'd feel better not sharing. Oh, I'm so embarrassed."

"No, please don't be. I'm sure he'll tell me some time if he wants to."

Sarah looked relieved. "All my children are special to me, but Arthur really does have a heart of gold."

Sarah left the kitchen and Chloe stayed behind to rearrange some cranberry brie bites that didn't need rearranging. She hadn't forgotten the conversation she had overheard at the wedding between Arthur and his brother. Arthur had said that he wasn't always alone at the farm. It had been an offhand comment, but she felt that there was something significant behind it. Was it related to his "big disappointment"?

Right beside the question about what would have happened that Sarah assumed was newsworthy enough to have gotten around town, there was also Chloe's guilt about agreeing to that date with Drake. It wasn't a real date; it was a way for her to get financing for the shop that she still felt she couldn't tell her friends about. Maybe it would be kinder to Arthur if she showed her true colors before they got too involved, especially if he was as sincere as he seemed and had already suffered some kind of great loss.

Or maybe Chloe still had a chance to redirect before it was too late. She hadn't done anything at all, not yet.

In the living room, the music was starting up, and Chloe rushed in and sat down. Scenes flashed by of beautiful towns all around the United States. There were mountains and oceans, fields and rivers, barns and restaurants. A child picked a ripe tomato; a man seared a steak in a pan; a smiling woman in a flowing skirt leaned over to pat a goat.

"That was me!" Bea cried, tears springing to her eyes.

"If we're going to start crying already, we're in trouble. I only have one box of tissues." Chloe passed one to her weepy friend.

The episode began with all four women seated around Bea's kitchen table. They discussed their society and their vision for the future of women in farming. Each time one of them spoke, images were shown of her life: her farm, animals, family, tools, and crops.

Each of their homes was visited as well. Lindsay and Grace gave a tour of their farmhouse turned bed and breakfast. It had been in their family since it was built in the 1880s by their great-great grandparents, who were Walloon Belgian immigrants. Sarah cooked rice pudding in her kitchen and prayed in her chapel. Bea demonstrated how the summer kitchen was used to bake bread and pies during the hottest months of the year. Chloe dug in her garden, tweaked designs on her computer, and snipped a branch with her pruning shears.

The way the documentary was pieced together led even Chloe, who had lived here almost all her life, to see familiar places in a new light. Why hadn't she noticed how beautiful everything was, how interconnected? There was Emma's Café, St. Mary of the Snows Church, the old cemetery, the one room schoolhouse, and the people, especially the people. Was she crying too? Impossible. She wiped the non-tears away with a tissue of her own.

There was Tom, who had pulled them out of the mud just the other day. He sat on a bench outside of Emma's Café with his fellow retired farmers, recounting stories of the good old days. Inside the café, Emma zoomed by with trays of delicacies. Betsy handed cherry stuffed waffles to a table full of Girl Scouts. Connie, the long-time librarian, gave a tour of the now defunct historic library while Wes looked on, stepping back to let her have her moment in the sun. The documentary ended with Kermiss, the annual Belgian harvest festival.

When it was over, they all clapped and

cheered. "We did it," Chloe cried. "We're amazing!"

"I am so proud of us. I wonder what everyone else thought," said Lindsay. "I don't know about you guys, but I'm tempted to run over there right away and see them."

"I am too," said Sarah. It was unanimous. They all agreed that it was time to head over to Sarah's to celebrate with their families.

When the women entered the old brick farmhouse, everyone was there to greet them. Chloe's mom ran over to her yelling, her arms in the air. She wrapped her in a hairspray and perfume scented hug. "Honey! You were incredible. I can't believe it. My own daughter, a famous designer. Who did your hair? You should style it like that more often."

Her dad stood behind her. "Very nice," he said, nodding his head.

"Thanks guys," said Chloe. "Your support has always meant a lot to me."

"Yup," her dad said, continuing to nod. They were both proud in their own way.

"Where's Betsy?" Chloe asked.

"She and George went out to celebrate afterwards," her mom said. "They might be back later."

Chloe was disappointed that she wouldn't be able to see her sister right away and a little concerned that Betsy was getting more deeply involved with George. She had mostly given up on worrying about them though. If their dance moves were any indication, they were having a fantastic time together. She looked around to see who else was there. Like maybe

Arthur, for instance.

Bea chatted with Wes and her dad by the fireplace. Lindsay and Grace excitedly discussed their favorite parts of the show. It sounded like Grace had come up with some new ideas during the documentary. Her creativity would go a long way towards helping Lindsay look forward to a brighter future.

Roy marched up to Chloe and slapped her on the back. "You're off to great places," he said. "That was quite the program for you ladies. Did you see my big moment?" She had. He kept walking behind Sarah while she was being interviewed, hauling boards or stretching. He did the same thing at Kermiss but with plates of food. "I never thought I'd see the day when Roy Watson was a famous actor. But at the same time, I've always believed that I would be discovered eventually. Better late than never, right?"

"You were fantastic," said Chloe.

"Yes. I was, wasn't I? You had a nice small part as well. Well done. I'm just happy that I could be the one to make this all happen for you. If it hadn't been for me telling the producer about your lady society, this day would never have come."

"That's a good point, Roy. This is your day. Enjoy it." She wouldn't fight with him. Besides, it was good practice. She silently thanked him for the challenge.

"I hear you and Georgie are going into business together," said Roy.

"I haven't agreed to anything yet, but we did talk about that recently." She wished that George hadn't told anyone about her possible involvement. It sounded like he considered it a sure thing already, but Chloe was certain that she had communicated her uncertainty, which had only grown since their day at Cana Island. If there was one thing you could say about George, it was that no one could ever accuse him of under-confidence.

"You can't go wrong teaming up with a guy like him. He's a rising star. He'll be taking anyone associated with him along for the ride. You should see the outfits he's set up in the cities."

"I agree. It's all very exciting. I just need to consider whether it's best for my business right now."

Arthur joined them, holding a glass cup covered with strawberries. So that's where he got those cute cups. "What are you two talking about?" he asked.

"This brilliant young woman is going into business with George," said Roy.

"I hadn't heard that." Arthur looked to Chloe for confirmation.

Her level headed consideration for Roy was diminishing by the minute. Couldn't he cut her a break? "Like I was telling your dad, we discussed the possibility. I may rent one of his shops, but it's not set in stone in any way." Arthur frowned and took a sip of his drink.

Roy wandered off, and Arthur asked Chloe if she wanted to take a walk around the farm. She considered whether the warmth of the house was worth the tradeoff of time alone with Arthur in the dark and cold. It was. Before sneaking out, she checked to make sure that no one was looking and pulled her jacket back on. They disappeared through the kitchen and out the back door.

"We're going to start to develop a reputation for sneaking off together," she said.

"I'm fine with that." He took her hand and they walked across the lawn. He led her to a bench that was hidden in a pretty copse of pine trees. They sat down together and she scooted close to him as he put his arm around her shoulder.

"Not to bring up a delicate subject, but have you given any thought to what happened the other night?" she asked.

"At the Halloween party? I've thought about it a lot. I'm not sorry that I kissed you. I'd even do it again. In fact, I'll do it right now." He did.

"I'm not sorry about that either," she said, nudging him. "But you know that's not what I'm talking about."

"I do. And I have thought about it. Sorry, I get jokey around awkward topics. I still can't believe we did that. Did you know that was a reporter's house?"

"I may have been familiar with where she lived. It's just too bad that Steve kept his mask on when she found him. I've been nervous that he's going to show up at my house now and get revenge. Do you think he knows that it was us?"

"I think I might be in the clear..."

"I know everyone suspects me," said Chloe. "How dare they? Why would I do such a thing?"

"You did do it though."

"Yeah, but people shouldn't assume."

"Well, I did an investigation of my own yesterday to see if I could discover anything more about what Steve's been up to."

She turned to look at him, but it was too dark to see clearly. She was touched that he had followed up like that. "You did?"

"Yes. Initially, I planned on leaving it alone. But that night, when I got home, I had a feeling that something else was amiss. I stopped by the feed store the next day and discreetly asked around to see if anyone had seen him lately."

"Didn't people think that was suspicious?"

"I don't think so. No one knows for sure who the gorilla man was. I've heard some amusing theories. We may have a spate of Sasquatch hunters in the area in the coming months."

"That's hilarious."

"Agreed. Anyway, I went to the feed store. I said that Steve used to come by the farm and that I hadn't seen him in a while. He did odd jobs, so he could've been over sometimes."

"What did they say?"

"One guy told me what we already knew, that he had moved up north and was renting a little house. Another guy said something strange, though. He lives out near Lindsay's, and he's seen Steve driving by at odd hours. He told me that he thought Steve and Lindsay might be making amends."

"They're clearly not. As far as Lindsay knows,

he hasn't been back since he left this summer, and now again at Halloween. What could he be doing out there?"

"I don't know. But like I said, something's not right."

"What should we do?" Chloe's nervous energy was begging to be released. She needed to take action. Maybe she could enlist the help of the Sasquatch hunters.

"I don't think there's anything we can do."

"Should we tell Lindsay?"

"You know her better than I do, but I think we should. I don't want to make too much out of this. It's possible there's an innocent explanation for the whole thing. But my gut says that something's off."

"Mine too," she said. "I don't want to turn Steve into some kind of a boogie man when he's most likely a run of the mill ne'er-do-well, but Lindsay should know that he may have been lurking around at other times without her knowledge. I'll talk to her soon. She was over before the documentary. I filled her in on what happened the other night."

"Is she ok?"

"She will be."

"She has good friends. Hey, I wanted to talk to you about something else," he said. "It's about you going into business with George."

"It's very tentative. He had planned an outing with an investor, but he cancelled at the last minute so I took his place. We kayaked out to the Cana Island lighthouse. He suggested that I might want to rent retail space, that's all."

"So you didn't give him money or anything?"

"No, I didn't, but that's a concerning question. Is there something I should know?"

Arthur rubbed his neck and Chloe took that as a yes. "Not really," he said. "I would advise caution, that's all."

"George has developed some successful properties, right?"

"He has. Yes. I don't want to badmouth him, not at all. I'm just saying that it might be a good idea to be careful. Don't get your hopes up too high. I've probably said too much as it is. I hope it works out for you."

"Are you sure there's not anything else?"

"Nope. Nothing else."

"Ok, but you're suggesting that I shouldn't invest any money with him."

"I didn't say that."

"It was implied."

"Fine. Yes. You shouldn't give him anything upfront."

"Do you want to tell me why?"

"He's not always reliable. That's all I'm going to say." He sounded as serious as she'd ever heard him.

Chloe wondered what he was omitting. Did he think that he couldn't trust her with sensitive information about his brother? Or was there really nothing more? Maybe he really was jealous of his brother's success. Would he begrudge her success as well?

If she had to choose between growing her business and being with Arthur, she thought she knew what side she would come down on. She had no interest in being with a man who needed her to dim her light to make him comfortable. She was heading into a murky situation, one that could lead to another entry in her famous list of ill-advised relationships.

This was all becoming too much: too many complications, too many decisions, and too many people who could either hurt her or be hurt by her. She was tempted to run away and hide from it all. For now though, she tried being direct. "My business is really important to me. I hope that's ok with you."

"Of course it is. Like I said, I hope it works out. I mean that."

That was nice to hear; she hoped it was true. "Also, I really like you. If you have any weird skeletons in your closet or in your walls or under your stairs or anything, you would tell me, right?" She wondered once again about his disappointment or breakup, or whatever it was.

"There are no skeletons in any of those places."

"Or anywhere else?"

He laughed. "No skeletons anywhere. I really like you too. In fact, I'm wondering if you'd like to go to a movie with me up north this Saturday night. They're playing Casablanca at the Sturgeon Bay Theater."

"This Saturday night?" She had plans with Drake. Plans that she knew she should never have made, but couldn't quite bring herself to cancel. The irony of grilling him about any skeletons in his closet while she agonized about one of her own was not lost on her. Her resolve was being tested. Would she choose Arthur or her business?

"I'm busy Saturday night. Another time though, ok?" The happiness she had felt moments before was replaced by a hollow feeling in the pit of her stomach. What if Arthur really was as amazing as he seemed? She didn't deserve him, but she wanted him.

She put her cold hands on his warm face and kissed. They stayed outside for a while, their frosty breath mingling in the November air.

Eventually, they stood up and went back to the house, walking in separately. They needn't have worried. No one noticed that they had been gone, but Bea gave Chloe a knowing look. Her rosy cheeks gave her away.

Chapter Seventeen

In Which Chloe is Surprisingly Restrained

The following morning, Chloe paced back and forth in her kitchen. Her papers were strewn across the table. What should she do? He hadn't said so directly, but she knew that Drake wouldn't even consider offering her a loan unless she agreed to a date with him. If she went on this one date though, where would it stop? Who's to say that he wouldn't keep asking for more? What else would she have to sacrifice in order to make her vision a reality?

She was tempted to dial Drake right now and call it all off. He would be in his office by now. Agreeing to dinner with him had been a mistake in the first place. Every time she picked up her phone, she pictured her beautiful shop slipping away. It was almost too much to bear. Maybe in this case, the ends would have to justify the means.

Chloe took Marshmallow outside to play fetch. She tossed the ball once and then gave up. Marshmallow couldn't have been happier with that arrangement. Into the grass next to the garden she sprawled, happily chomping on her ball.

Chloe sat down next to her to talk things

through. "I don't know what to do. I'm still not even sure that having a shop there is the right thing to do. Am I just in it for myself? It seems like everyone else is, and I won't get anywhere unless I play along... Not you, though."

Maybe not Arthur either, but she didn't want to cancel for his sake alone. She still thought there might be an issue there. He couldn't be as perfect as he seemed. Before she made any kind of a decision, she wanted to be sure that she was doing it for herself.

Marshmallow got up and trotted away with the ball in her mouth, obviously worried that it could be snatched away at any moment. Chloe would have to reason this out on her own. Maybe she could try going to another bank. She knew it was a bit of a stretch for her, but she was organized and motivated to succeed. Someone else might be willing to take a chance on her, and if they weren't willing to right now, she would work that much harder until they did.

She also considered the image she had presented in the documentary, and what it meant to her to empower other women to follow their dreams. How could she live with herself if she turned right around and allowed herself to be blackmailed by some sleazy guy?

She strode into the house, calling Marshmallow on her way, and picked up her phone. She brought up Drake's number and called him before she could change her mind. "Hello there beautiful," he said. The second she heard his voice, she knew that she was making the right decision. How could she have even considered accepting his offer?

"I'm busy Saturday. Don't worry about the loan, either. I'm taking my business elsewhere." She hung up before he could reply.

Chapter Eighteen

In Which a Villain Strikes

"How is it possible that you've never seen Casablanca before?" Arthur asked, handing Chloe a big tub of popcorn. She took a handful and passed it back.

"I'm not sure," she replied. "I've seen clips of it. I know the famous lines, but I never sat down and watched the whole thing."

"Well, you're in for a treat then."

"I believe it. It looks like those two, on the other hand, might miss out on some of the finer points of the film." She nodded to a couple at the front of the theater who were obviously more interested in each other than the trailers.

"Usually people sit in the back if that's their intention."

"Maybe they were unexpectedly overcome by passion."

"It's happened to the best of us..." said Arthur. He winked at her, looking just like George as he did.

The woman in the front row stood up and headed down the aisle towards them. She was blonde and pretty and related to Chloe. She couldn't believe her eyes. It was Betsy. Now that she looked more closely, the guy sitting in the front row with her had to be George.

Betsy was about to walk past them when her sister stepped into the aisle in front of her. "Surprise!"

"Ahh! What are you doing here?"

"I'm here to watch a movie. What are you here for?"

"You're a laugh riot. We're here for the movie too."

"I can tell you two are really into classic films. Are you going to get popcorn? I'll come with you." She followed Betsy out of the theater and they both got in line.

"So, it looks like you and George are a bit of an item now," said Chloe.

"An item? How old are you? No one says that."

"You know what I mean. Aren't you going to heed my sisterly wisdom at all? I know he's fun, but you must see that he's not serious. He probably has seven girlfriends back home."

"You're one to talk, 'sisterly wisdom'. You're here with his twin brother." Betsy was the next one up. She ordered popcorn and a soda.

"Arthur's different."

"Different how? You just think he's better because you're here with him. Or are you jealous that George didn't pick you?" She walked away.

Chloe scampered along behind her, keeping a bit of distance between them. She hadn't forgotten Betsy's propensity to fling drinks at people that she disagreed with. "I am not jealous at all. I just know how attached you get to people right away, and I'm suggesting that it might be more prudent to maintain some emotional distance."

Betsy spun around to face her. "I'm not going to push him away on the off chance that it won't work out."

"I'd say there's more than an off chance that it's not going to work out."

Betsy turned back around and marched into the theater. Right before she sat down next to George she gave Chloe a wave. If a wave could ever be considered sarcastic, this one was. Arthur looked straight ahead and addressed his date out of the corner of his mouth. "Is everything alright?"

"It's fine. I'm a little nervous about those two. It's not just your brother." She didn't want to offend him. "It's Betsy too. I think that one of them is going to get hurt sooner rather than later."

"I'm not offended. I agree. At the same time though, they'll figure it out. I doubt this is unfamiliar territory for either of them. It seems like they're enjoying each other's company."

"That's what I'm worried about," said Chloe. The lights dimmed and the music started. The black and white movie began. Chloe absolutely loved everything about it. She loved the music, the costumes, and the star-crossed lovers.

"Hey Arthur," she said, halfway through the movie. "I have a question."

"Shoot." His eyes were glued to the screen.

"Are we dating? I realize we're on a date right

now, but what if someone else asked you out? What would you say?"

"I would say no."

"No because you're dating me?"

"Yes." He turned to face her, leaning in to whisper in her ear. "I don't date much. If I'm with you, it's because I want to be with you. I think you're perfect for me." He went back to watching the movie, like he hadn't just said the sweetest thing anyone had ever said to her.

Chloe shifted in her seat. She wasn't perfect, not at all. She said the wrong things, she was judgmental, and she had considered going on a date with someone else just to advance her career. Maybe it would be kinder to let him see her, warts and all, so he wouldn't waste anymore of his time.

They watched the rest of the movie in silence, staying in their seats while the credits rolled. By the end of the movie, Chloe was so enthralled that she had forgotten all about her self recrimination. She gushed about the movie until the lights came back on, and it was revealed that they were the only ones left in the theater. Their respective siblings had already gone.

"I like coming to the really late movies because you almost always have the whole theater to yourself," said Arthur. "It's kind of funny that my brother had the same idea."

Chloe agreed. "It was like a double date. And speaking of dates, I'm dating you too." She thanked her lucky stars that she had chosen to go to the movie with him.

"Good to hear it. I guess we're dating each other then. That's convenient. Want to take the scenic route back?" he asked as they walked outside. It was another clear cold night. The stars were streaked and spattered across the cloudless sky and the moon was nearly full.

"Yes. Let's do that," she said. They walked to Arthur's truck and drove away. He soon turned onto the county road that would take them on a winding path home. He flipped on some country music, a song about a man who was saying goodbye to his old tractor.

"I think we have a theme going tonight," he said, "between the movie and the song, lovers parting. I'm a little more affected by the story of the man with his tractor, but it's situational. My tractor and I are close."

"It's good to know where I stand, but I'm going to have to give my vote to Casablanca," Chloe replied.

"So I take it you liked the movie?"

"I did, most of it anyway."

"What part weren't you sure about?"

"Well, the more that I consider it, the more I wonder about something. Wouldn't it have been better if Humphrey Bogart and Ingrid Bergman had ended up together in the end? They were meant to be. They were clearly still mad about each other. They shouldn't have let anything stand in their way."

"I'm not so sure. She had made her choice long before they even met. It had always been too late."

"It's never too late. You're so practical."

"I don't know if practicality has anything to do with it. They couldn't have been truly happy together, knowing that she had abandoned her prison-of-war husband."

"It's so sad though."

"I don't mean to be contrarian, but I don't think of it as sad at all. It's what real love is all about. That's why it's a classic. In other movies, the characters will do whatever it takes just to be together. It's simple to please people that way. In Casablanca, though, they love each other so much that they would rather do the right thing than be together... This way goes past Lindsay's house, doesn't it?" Arthur asked. They passed rolling hills and quiet farmhouses.

"It does. I'd suggest we stop by to say hi, but given that it's one in the morning, she'll definitely be asleep."

They slowed down as they turned the bend that lay right before Lindsay's bed and breakfast. They passed a black pickup truck on the shoulder of the road, and Chloe did a double take.

"Stop," she said.

Arthur hit the brakes. "What is it?"

"I think that might've been Steve's truck back there. Can you turn around?"

He did. He parked behind the truck.

Chloe hopped out. She knew it was his already, but she wanted to be sure that her mind wasn't playing tricks on her. She'd been hyper vigilant ever since she heard that it was possible that he was still snooping around. It was his alright. A small scratch on the passenger side was the final confirmation.

Getting back into Arthur's truck, she turned to face him. "That has to be Steve's."

Arthur scanned the dark field. "What do you think he's doing here? Could he and Lindsay be up talking?"

"At one in the morning? It's not impossible, but it seems really unlikely. Besides, why would he have parked so far down the road?"

"Good point. Why don't we check if there are any lights on in the house?"

"I'll try calling her on the way." Arthur pulled back onto the road while Chloe tried Lindsay's phone. She didn't answer. "I'll try texting her." She sent her a message asking if she was awake, not wanting to say more and scare her in case she didn't know that Steve was around. "She's not responding."

Arthur pulled into the driveway. The red brick farmhouse was almost completely dark except for a dim light coming from the kitchen. "What should we do?" Arthur asked. "I don't want to intrude."

"Something's not right. The chances of me peeking in that window to see Steve and Lindsay having a coffee clutch at one in the morning are slim to none."

"I think we should go up and check it out. What if he's in there right now while Lindsay and Grace are asleep upstairs?"

"You're right. We can catch him in the act and

figure out what he's up to."

They climbed out of the truck and closed the doors gently. They padded up the driveway and climbed the back stairs to the kitchen. Chloe hoisted herself on the railing and peeked in the window next to the back door.

"Careful," said Arthur, hanging onto her legs so she didn't tumble off.

"I don't see anyone inside." She gripped the windowsill. "There's a light on over the sink, but they might leave that on overnight."

"Where is he?"

Nothing moved in the frosty orchard. The door to the summer kitchen was sealed shut and leaves had gathered across the threshold, suggesting that no one had entered it in quite some time. The garage was dark and quiet as well. What about the barn? She glanced directly behind her. The barn door was slightly ajar. Had Lindsay accidentally left it open, or was there someone inside? Chloe nodded towards the open door and hopped down.

"What next?" Arthur received no reply. Chloe was already running down the stairs and across the yard. He sprinted to catch up.

When they got there, Chloe sneaked up to the door, ready to leap in and surprise that sneaky scoundrel. Instead, she sniffed the air. "Do you smell something burning?"

Arthur flung open the door. They were overwhelmed by billowing smoke. Flames leapt on the other side of the barn. Chloe coughed as she sprinted inside.

"What are you doing? We need to get out," Arthur called, following behind and pulling her in the direction of the exit and safety.

She yanked her arm away. "Just a minute. I know where the fire extinguisher is. I just have to think."

"No. You're not doing this. We're leaving. Now."

She ran towards the fire, crouching low to avoid the smoke, and spotted a fire extinguisher attached to the wall in the far corner of the barn. "Found it!" she cried. "Go! Call 911."

Arthur ran forward. "I'm not leaving without you. Come on."

"I think the fire's still small enough for me to put it out," she said. "I have to try." She took aim and sprayed the base of the flames. The smoke slowed, but it still filled the barn. She dropped the empty fire extinguisher, turned around, and darted outside with Arthur. Bending over with her hands on her knees, she took in a freezing lungful of clean air.

"I can't believe you," said Arthur. "You could've been killed."

"I'm sorry. I had to try," she said. She rubbed her stinging eyes. He pulled her into his arms and they both peered into the yard, checking for any sign of Steve. Chloe's vision was blurry with tears.

Arthur headed back to his truck. "Call the police. I'm going to drive over there and see if I can head him off."

"Please don't. He could be dangerous. Who knows what's going through his mind right now?"

"I can't just let him get away. He could've killed somebody." He drove away and Chloe called the police, reporting what happened. The fire department would be there soon too. Chloe leaped up the stairs and banged on Lindsay's door until she answered.

"What's wrong?" asked Lindsay groggily.

"I need you to come out here. There was a fire in the barn."

"What? No!"

"I think it's out but we should..."

Lindsay darted past her and ran down the steps in her bare feet. She opened the barn door as Chloe ran up behind her. The barn was still full of smoke.

"It looks like it's out," said Chloe. The wall was charred and it smelled terrible, like burning plastic. Lindsay looked like she was debating whether she should go inside.

She lifted alternating feet to keep them from freezing in the icy grass.

"What happened?" she asked. "What were you doing here?"

"Arthur and I took the scenic route home after a movie in Sturgeon Bay and saw Steve's truck on the road near your driveway."

"What was he doing there?"

"He wasn't in the truck when we got there; Arthur's going to see if he can find him now."

"You don't think...he couldn't..."

Chloe didn't know what to say.

"So what happened next? How did you know to look in the barn?" Lindsay asked.

"We peeked in your window, sure that something weird was going on. I found the barn door open, ran in, and put the fire out."

"Thank you. I'm so grateful to you, but I hope you were careful. My barn is important to me, sure, but if anything had happened to you..." Lindsay couldn't finish her sentence. "When is this going to be over?"

She pulled her robe over her head and screamed into it for a while. Popping out, she said, "Do you mind if we go back inside? I'm freezing."

As they walked in the back door, Grace clomped down the stairs with her eyes half shut. "What are you guys doing?"

"Steve tried to burn down the barn," said Lindsay.

"You're kidding." She looked between the two of them. Their faces were drawn and serious. "No way. That can't be true. This is like a nightmare. Is everyone ok?"

"Everyone is fine. Chloe ran in there like a mad woman and put out the fire."

"How did you know it was him?" Grace asked.

They sat down at the table and explained everything again. "He has completely lost his mind," said Grace. "This is so scary."

"It makes sense though, in a twisted way." Lindsay stared at the table with tired eyes. She sagged in her seat.

"What do you mean?" Chloe asked.

"He owns half of everything here, so I'm going to have to find a way to give him half the value of all of this. It's going to be tough. We've put a ton of work into the barn, and it's a huge part of the business. It's insured for a crazy amount of money, because it would be so expensive to replace everything from scratch. If we got the insurance money, half of it would be his, and I wouldn't have a barn anymore."

As they sat there, looking at each other in shock, the sound of blaring sirens cut through the silence. Arthur walked in the back door, and all three women were startled out of their seats.

"It's just me!" he said, holding up his hands and pulling down his hood. "It's like I thought, there was no sign of him. His truck is gone. He even swept up the tire marks in the gravel where he was parked. He'll have quite a surprise when he finds out that the barn is still standing."

There was a knock at the door. It was Officer Anselme. "The fire department is in the barn right now," he said. "It looks like the fire is out. I'm going to need to take statements from all of you."

They told him what had happened, including their suspicions about Steve's motive for attempting to burn down the barn. "We have word out to officers in this and neighboring counties on the lookout for his vehicle. We'll try to locate him tonight or first thing tomorrow morning for questioning, and the fire marshal will be here in the morning to investigate. Please don't go anywhere near the scene. Do you have someone who can stay with you tonight?"

Arthur spoke up right away. "I'll stay."

"Me too," Chloe said.

The officer went outside and all four of them sat down again. "I don't know how to thank you two," Lindsay said her friends. "I'm grateful that we don't have any lodgers tonight. I can't imagine what they would think about all this. The thought of waking up to a burned down ban though..."

Chloe couldn't imagine what that moment would have been like for her friend. What were the chances that she and Arthur had just happened to take the scenic route home? It could have so easily gone differently.

That barn had been a special place for all of them since they were girls, even before it was restored. They used to put on plays there and choreograph dances, inviting their friends and family to watch them. She recalled the first time she noticed Arthur's charms, when they had sipped cider there not long ago. She remembered Hannah's beautiful wedding and the fabulous Halloween party. Thanks to dumb luck, and maybe a touch of something more, there would be many happy moments to come.

Out of nowhere, a thought occurred to her. "The barn was full of smoke, but the smoke alarms weren't going off."

"I wondered about that too," said Lindsay. "They're programmed to wake us up and alert the fire department."

"Could Steve have disconnected them?"

"He must have. I won't be able to rest easy until he's caught."

"Me either," said Grace.

It was a long night. The police came in and out, asking questions and taking notes. Finally, Grace fell asleep at the table and she and Lindsay went up to bed. Chloe doubted that either of them would get much sleep. She knew she wouldn't. Arthur offered to stay on the couch so that someone was downstairs. They climbed the stairs together to get blankets and a pillow out of the cabinet.

"You saved the day," Arthur said. "I wish I would've caught him."

"It's ok. You tried, and really, what could you have done if you had?"

"I have no idea. It just irks me that he got away when he must've been so close."

"I'm grateful that you went after him, but I have no doubt that the police will track him down. He can't have gone far. He may not even know that he was discovered yet."

They went downstairs and made Arthur a bed on the couch. He climbed under the covers and closed his eyes. Chloe tiptoed away, taking one backwards glance before she left the room.

Chapter Nineteen

In Which a Sick Day Provides Revelations

The following morning, Chloe woke up in one of Lindsay's guest bedrooms. She made the bed, gently pulling the patchwork quilt over the mattress, and tiptoed downstairs. Peeking outside at the barn, she saw that most of the police and firefighters were gone now. There was one police car in the driveway and she guessed that there was probably an officer inside, securing the crime scene and waiting for the fire marshal.

Soft morning light filled the kitchen. In the light of day, the ominous feeling that had overcome her last night diminished, but its residue remained. She poured herself a glass of water and peeked into the living room.

Arthur wasn't on the couch. The blankets were folded neatly, topped with his pillow. She heard the sink running in the bathroom. He walked out and stretched.

"Good morning," he said. "That was quite a night."

"You can say that again. It doesn't seem like it really happened. Have you seen Lindsay or Grace?"

"They must still be asleep."

"I'm glad. I expected to see them both up at the kitchen table already this morning."

"They probably didn't get much sleep. I wish I could stick around to talk to them, but I have to get back to my cows."

"I have to get back too. Thanks again for staying last night."

"I wouldn't have had it any other way."

"I'm just going to leave a note for Lindsay before we go."

Chloe went back into the kitchen and rummaged in the drawers until she found a piece of paper. She wrote that she'd be back later and left the note on the table. Arthur joined her, pulling on his jacket, and she followed him out the door. On the way back in home, they were both quiet, lost in thought.

"Do you think they've caught him yet?" Chloe asked.

"I hope so," he said. "I'm getting a little burnt out on keeping up with this guy."

"Agreed. Do you still feel conflicted about Halloween night?"

"Not at all. Any concern I had about it has evaporated completely. I still can't believe how you saved Lindsay's barn. You spotted his truck too."

"You ran after him though. See? You are my accomplice," said Chloe.

"It appears that you use your considerable powers for good, so I'm happy to accept the role."

Arriving home, Chloe got out of the truck and

waved goodbye as Arthur drove away. She and Marshmallow took a walk and ate breakfast, and then she headed back over to Lindsay's. When she got there, more cars were parked in the driveway. She backed up to the shoulder of the road and went inside.

Lindsay and Grace sat at the kitchen table now, drinking tea and talking. Chloe pulled up a chair and joined them. "They haven't found Steve yet," said Lindsay. "They won't tell me anything beyond that. They were just in here, asking all kinds of questions. I feel like I'm a suspect myself."

"I'm sure it's just standard procedure," said Chloe. "Steve obviously did it. Where could he have gone?"

"I wonder the same thing. It's like he disappeared. I probably would have assumed that it was an accident, if it wasn't for you and Arthur."

Chloe got a text from Betsy. She was feeling sick and wouldn't be able to go to their painting event that evening.

"That's too bad," said Grace. "She was really looking forward to going. She talks about you all the time."

"She does?" She had the feeling that Betsy was irritated with her lately, especially after their encounter last night. Maybe she wasn't even really sick...

"You don't have to stay," said Lindsay. "I can't even begin to tell you how much I appreciate all your help, but there's not much more to do here right now. I'm so drained."

"Alright. Hang in there." Chloe got up to leave. "I'm only a phone call away though." She stepped outside and took a moment to appreciate the beautiful old barn, grateful that it was still standing.

When she got in her truck, she called Betsy. "Hey, you feeling sick?"

"Yes. I'm sorry. I really wanted to go. Will you still come over tonight though?" So Betsy really did want to spend time with her.

"Of course. You sound awful. I don't want to bother you."

"You won't be bothering me. I'm bored already."

"See you tonight then." They hung up. She was touched. Last night must have been forgotten. She wasn't sure if she should tell Betsy about the awful scene after the movie, given that she wasn't feeling well. Betsy would find out soon enough though.

The day passed in a blur of emails and phone calls. By the time Chloe got to her sister's house that evening, she was ready for a break from thinking and talking about her tools. Betsy was tucked under a blanket on her couch. Her head was propped up with piles of pillows and she clutched a blanket under her chin.

"Why do I have to feel so awful?" she said, blowing her nose and groaning. She tossed a tissue into the wastebasket, and Chloe handed her a cup of hot lemon water. Betsy took a sip and handed it back. "Thanks for coming over. It's so depressing to be home alone when you're sick."

"Any time," said Chloe. "Remember when I had the flu, and you walked my dog for me?"

Betsy leaned back and closed her eyes. "Yes. She pulled me into the road, and I slipped on the ice." The lab propped her front paws on the couch and licked Betsy's face. "Yes. I'm talking about you, crazy dog." Marshmallow flopped back down and sighed. "I really wanted to go to that painting party, too."

"I think there'll be another one next month. I bet she'll even have a Christmas project. We can plan on going then." Wes's mom, who was an artist, had started holding monthly get-togethers in which she provided canvases, paint, instruction, and food for an evening of fun.

"Yeah. You're right. It was a good idea though," said Betsy.

"It was a great idea. I was excited to hear that you were thinking about picking up painting again." Chloe sat down on the big chair next to the couch and grabbed her own mug of tea. She stirred the honey at the bottom and it swirled and melted away.

"I really just wanted to spend more time with you." Betsy sat up taller and coughed a bit.

"Me? I thought I was boring."

"Are you kidding? They just made a documentary about you. They wouldn't do that if you were boring."

"It was about my ergonomic tools, though. That doesn't exactly make me exciting. You're the cool one. You've got the dance moves and the fun friends."

"I have fun, sure, but I've always looked up to you. I want to hang out with you. You, Lindsay, and Bea are always doing interesting things. You have been since we were kids. I tried to tag along, but you shooed me away."

"I guess I never thought about it like that. I was kind of nerdy. You were always the popular one. You still are." Chloe considered it some more. "I guess I did tell you to leave us alone a lot when we were younger."

She hadn't wanted her little sister tagging along with her and her friends. Now, though, she loved spending time with her and wished she had realized what a lovely person she was all along.

She also recalled the sarcastic comments she had made over the years about Betsy's boyfriends, including the one about George last night. In fact, she often disapproved of what Betsy was doing or who she was with, and she wasn't shy about telling her so. Maybe Chloe wasn't the model sister she so often told herself she was. "I meant to say something before. The bachelorette party you planned for Hannah was so thoughtful. She really loved it."

"Really? I had a blast, but I wasn't sure if it was ok."

"Absolutely. It was perfect."

"You didn't think I went overboard?"

"Not at all. It was really creative and personal. You did an amazing job. Did you notice that she sneaked the James Dean poster into her trunk at the end of the night?"

"I did notice that." Betsy held back a laugh and coughed again. "I was going to give it to her anyway. I wonder where she put it. Her new husband might be freaked out if she hangs it up in their bedroom."

Chloe laughed too. She hated to bring up a negative subject, but she had avoided it up until now. "Hey, this is really unrelated, but I have to tell you something."

"It sounds serious. Are you ok?"

"It's about last night."

"Oh. Don't worry about it. I get it. George gives off the impression of being a reckless heartbreaker, but he's really a sweetheart."

"It's not about George..." Chloe told her all about what happened after the movie.

"No way," said Betsy. "Grace was never crazy about Steve, not even when he and Lindsay were dating. She never said anything about it, though. She feels guilty about that now."

"It's not her fault. It's his. I just hope they catch him soon so he won't be able to bother Lindsay for a very long time."

Betsy picked up her phone and scrolled. "It looks like he wouldn't be able to bother her for a minimum of six years, and he has to pay for three times the damages."

Chloe stood up and took the mugs into the kitchen. "Do you mind if I do the dishes? Do you need anything?"

"Have at 'em. I'm fine though. Thanks. I'm going to try to take a nap."

"Let me know if Marshmallow is bothering you."

"She's never bothering anyone, are you?" Betsy said. The dog stood up and gave her a lick on the cheek.

Chloe went into the kitchen and filled the sink with soapy water. She washed the mugs, admiring the canvas on the wall above the table. Two cows grazed in a field, their heads hanging low. Betsy had painted them in high school. The colors were bold and unexpected, nothing like real life, but they harmonized together in a way that made sense. Chloe shook the bubbles off her hands and peeked into the living room. It looked like the patient had fallen asleep already.

Marshmallow popped up and wagged her tail. She started to bark and Chloe shushed her. Someone was parking next to the curb in front of the house. She couldn't tell who it was in the dark.

Chloe went outside to greet the person so he wouldn't knock on the door and wake her sister. It was George. He was leaning over to grab something from the passenger seat. He stood up and turned around, clutching a bouquet of sunflowers and a Tupperware of soup. "I'll have to come out for the rest of it," he said.

"I can carry something," Chloe offered. He handed her a pile of movies and she tried to hide her surprise. It wouldn't be much fun for him to hang out with Betsy while she was sick. "That was so thoughtful of you. She'll love it. She's sleeping right now, but come on in. I was just finishing up the dishes."

They tiptoed into the house and George and Marshmallow followed Chloe into the kitchen. He put the soup in the fridge and got out a vase for the flowers. He seemed comfortable in Betsy's kitchen, like he had been there before.

"This must be Marshmallow," he said, kneeling down and giving her a scratch behind the ears. "I've heard so much about you. You're a good girl." George stood up and the dog gazed at him adoringly before wandering back into the living room. "How's Betsy feeling? She sounded terrible on the phone."

"She's really stuffed up," Chloe said. "It's strange to see her like this. She's hardly ever sick."

"We'll have her feeling better in no time. I brought those cookies that she likes from Emma's too, the white chocolate cherry ones." Once again, Chloe was taken aback by him, but not in the way that she was used to. "I'll run out to the car and grab them."

"George?" Betsy called from the other room, "Is that you?"

He left the kitchen. Chloe took out the garbage through the side door to give them some time alone. When she got back inside, he had moved the flowers from the kitchen to the coffee table next to Betsy. He was back in the car getting the rest of her treats.

"How do I look?" Betsy asked. Truthfully, her red nose stood out against her pallid face, her hair was lank, and her eyes were puffy.

"You look great," Chloe said.

"Oh good. George said he was coming over, but I didn't think he really would. Who wants to hang out with a sick person?"

"Well, I did but…"

"I know, and I appreciate it so much. I've never had a guy do that for me before though. It's like he really cares, you know?"

"Yeah. I do." It made her sad that her sister was so taken aback that someone she was dating took an interest in her when she wasn't being entertaining. George walked back in with a stack of movies, holding a white bakery bag under his arm.

"Are those what I think they are?" Betsy asked.

"I thought they might cheer you up." He went into the kitchen and brought out a cookie on a plate. Betsy sat up and devoured it.

"Thank you so much," she said. "I'm feeling better already. My two favorite people are here."

"Do you want to watch a movie?" George asked. He fanned them out in front of her.

"The Princess Bride, Billy Madison, and My Best Friend's Wedding are all my favorites. I want to watch them equally. Mix them up and I'll close my eyes and pick one." He did and she picked Princess Bride.

"I should go," said Chloe. She didn't want to be in the way.

"Stay here," said Betsy. "This is one of your favorites too. Or it used to be, before you got all cynical on me."

"I may still be a little bit of a romantic," said Chloe. George sat down at one end of the couch and rubbed Betsy's feet.

He had just gone one step too far. "Do you mind

if I look in your trunk?" Chloe asked. George looked confused.

"Chloe!" Betsy said.

"I'm kidding. I'm only kidding."

Chapter Twenty

In Which a Letter Delivers Unexpected News

The following morning, Chloe was working at her kitchen table when she heard frantic pounding at her front door. She jumped up, ran over, and flung it open. It was her younger sister, still looking awful. She rubbed her tear streaked face, exposing a crumpled letter that she held in her fist. "What's wrong?" Chloe asked.

"It's George. He left me this..." Betsy shoved the letter into Chloe's hand, pushed into the living room, and flopped down onto the couch face first.

"What does it say? Is he alright?" Chloe asked.

"He must have slid it under my door this morning. I found it when I woke up." Betsy didn't lift her head. "Just read it."

My Dearest Betsy,

My heart is breaking as I write these words, but I must move on. I can't take it any longer. My brother's interference in my life has become too much for me to bear. Last night, after I visited you at home, Arthur came out to see me out at our parents' house. He told me that my association with you and your family had caused him too much embarrassment. He said that he tried to keep his relationship with Chloe a secret, and that my indiscretion was ruining our family's reputation. He objected principally to your mother, but he also alluded to some trouble that you had gotten into in recent months. He and I have been down this road before. He is jealous of me and my accomplishments. I know him too well. If I don't go along with his every whim, he will make the remainder of my time here miserable. I wish there was a way for us to be together, but here is where I say goodbye. Please don't look for me. The sooner we accept the truth, the easier it will be to move on.

All My Love,
George

Chloe lowered the letter and looked at Betsy. "I'm so sorry. This is all my fault."

"What do you mean? It's Arthur's fault. He's jealous. George told me all about it. This has happened before. It's so unfair." Her voice came out muffled as she pressed her face into a folded up throw pillow.

"No. Arthur tried to warn me about this. He told me that George wasn't trustworthy. The signs were there, but I hadn't wanted to see them. I wanted

George to be above board, partly because I'd become so attached to the idea of having a shop, but there was more to it than that."

"What does it matter? You tried to warn me too. You were right. He's gone and he's never coming back."

Chloe sat on the edge of the couch next to her sister. "I feel like a fool."

"That makes two of us." Betsy popped up. "You said there was another reason you wanted to believe in George?"

"There was. It gave me an excuse to think that Arthur himself wasn't all he was cracked up to be. It was easier for me to think that his warning was sour grapes, because then I would've been right to keep some emotional distance."

Even now, Chloe felt that underlying current of doubt. Could Arthur be embarrassed to be seen with her family? Her mom had made that speech at Hannah's wedding. And she could be a little flamboyant. Maybe a lot flamboyant sometimes, but who was he to judge? He had Roy, and George was no wallflower.

She reread the part about Arthur keeping his relationship with her a secret. That had a ring of truth to it as well. They hadn't exactly been public with their new relationship. He had taken her to a really late movie. They went hunting in the middle of nowhere. They walked through the orchard a couple of times and sneaked away at his house.

It didn't make sense though. Why would he have bothered to spend any time with her at all if he didn't want to be associated with her family? Like he had said himself, he wasn't the kind of guy to date around just for the fun of it. He seemed thoughtful and considerate. Chloe really didn't believe that he would do that to her. George, on the other hand…If she had to decide whether to put her faith in Arthur or George, she would choose Arthur every time. This would be easily sorted out. She'd show the letter to Arthur and hear what he had to say.

Either George was lying or his twin was an exceptional actor. If Arthur really was making someone else's life miserable out of jealousy, she didn't know him as well as she thought she did. Maybe this was his fatal flaw, finally coming to the surface. Or maybe George was a shady and insufferable rogue. There was only one way to find out.

"What are we going to do?" Betsy asked.

"Wait here. I'm going over to talk to Arthur right now."

"Give him a piece of your mind."

"I'm just going to ask him about this. Something doesn't add up here."

Betsy went back to crying and Chloe hung onto the crumpled letter, heading over to Arthur's house. She didn't know what to think. At the very least Arthur would be able to speak to the accusations leveled against him.

She was so disappointed. She had finally found someone that she was really growing to care about, and now it was all falling apart. Poor Betsy, no matter what happened she was going to be crushed. George sure had left town in a hurry too. Was he really that intimidated by the threat of his brother's disapproval?

Chloe pulled into Arthur's driveway. She ran up his front steps and rapped on the door. It took a while, but he eventually answered. He looked tired and disheveled, an unusual state of affairs for him. A stubbly shadow covered half his face and there were bags under his eyes.

"Hi," he said. "Come on in." He hadn't noticed Chloe's severe expression yet. She walked past him and, as he turned to face her, his smile faded away. "Are you ok?"

"Not particularly. Betsy received a letter from George this morning." She held it out to him, watching his face.

He appeared to understand right away. "He had to leave town unexpectedly," he said, as if that explained anything. He smoothed the letter out between his hands.

"Would you mind telling me why? That letter contains his side of the story, but I'm afraid it doesn't paint you in a very flattering light."

"What?" he asked. "I don't know what you mean." He looked down at the letter.

"Read it for yourself," said Chloe.

Arthur did read it then, his face impassive. When he got to the end of it, he crumpled it back up in his hand. He shook his head. "I'm sorry for Betsy. I expected better from my brother. None of this is true. Do you mind if I keep it?"

"I'd like it back, please," she said. He reluctantly handed it back to her. "Which part isn't true? Are you embarrassed to be seen with me?"

"No, not even a little bit. I'd happily be seen with you anywhere. I think your family is great. It's nothing like that."

"Are you jealous of George?"

"Not at all."

She shoved the note in her pocket. "What is it then? Has he really left town for good? He won't be coming back? He claims that you two had a falling out a few years ago over something like this, and he had to leave then too."

"He does, does he? It seems like he's covered all his bases. I'm sorry. I don't want to get into any of this. I can't tell you why he left. All I will say is that he is gone and no, he's not coming back. Everything else in that letter is a complete fabrication."

"That's it? You refuse to tell me why he left either time?"

"Yes. I'm sorry. I can't tell you."

"And I'm just supposed to believe you about everything else?"

"Yes. You're supposed to believe me."

She threw up her hands. "But why won't you trust me enough to tell me what's going on?"

"It's not my place to tell. The letter makes it clear that he doesn't want anyone to know the truth, least of all Betsy. I wouldn't either, if I were him. He's my brother. He left, and that's all anyone needs to know."

"Well, Betsy's my sister and she's going to be devastated. What am I supposed to tell her?"

"I don't know. I'm sorry."

"Well so am I." Chloe heard a door slam at the back of the house. "Is someone here?"

"Tom's helping me with my greenhouse. I better head back."

"So that's it?"

"What do you mean?"

"I mean, that's it between us. You're not going to tell me what happened with George, and you can't explain why he would say that you disapprove of my family."

"No. I'm not going to tell you. All I can say is that I like you. I would be proud to be seen with you anywhere. I don't want it to be over between us, and I'd like you to trust me."

Chloe took a deep breath. She didn't want to let him go. It would've been great if they could just forget about this and move on, but she was done with conveniently ignoring issues in her relationships. "I'm sorry. I don't think I can do that."

"Then I'm sorry too. I really do care about you."

Not enough to tell me the truth. "Goodbye Arthur."

He turned around and headed out the back door. Chloe sagged back to her truck, yanked the letter out of her pocket, and ripped it down the middle. She should've known that it wouldn't last.

On her way home, she passed her dad's shop.

Before she could consider the wisdom of the idea, she found herself parking her truck and walking inside.

"Hey Dad," said Chloe. She sat down on a chair along the wall.

He rolled out from under a truck. "Hey. Can you help me out under here? Karl's out sick today, and I'm falling behind."

"Sure," she said, pulling on a pair of coveralls.

"Will you hand me that socket wrench?" he asked.

She passed it over and slid under the truck next to him. "This truck is in every other week," he said. "I keep telling him it's not a tank, but he insists on driving anywhere and everywhere."

"Can I talk to you about something?" Chloe asked.

"Go ahead. Is it about Old Blue?"

"No, Old Blue is fine. It's about..." She considered how to broach the subject without causing him to shut down completely. She was just going to have to go for it. She told him about Betsy's letter from George and what it said. She told him about her conversation with Arthur.

Her dad kept working. Just as she had begun to fear that he might not say anything at all, he spoke. "No one is perfect. Not you, not anyone."

"I know that but..."

"I don't know if you do," he said, handing back the wrench. "I haven't always been the greatest dad or husband. I could've done more to guide you girls. Your mom and I have had some challenges that I decided not to own up to. And most importantly, I haven't told you ladies how much you mean to me. You all drive me crazy sometimes, but I wouldn't have it any other way."

"You did what you could. We know how you feel, Dad."

"I'm not telling you this so you can tell me what a great job I've done. I'm telling you so you'll hear me out when I point out your shortcomings too."

"Oh."

"Yup. I was just getting to them. As I was saying, I stuck my head in the sand more often than was good for all of us, during the good times and the bad. I know that. But there's also something to be said for accepting that life is messy. People are messy."

"I realize that, but I can't accept just anything."

"That's not what I'm suggesting at all. But you can accept more things. Make note of the good things that you do and the positives in other people. You have a lot of great people in your life, but you're going to be lonely and disappointed if you can't do that."

Chloe did feel lonely. So many people had let her down, including herself.

"I don't know what happened with George," he said, "but if he's decided to leave, it's probably best to let him be. Your sister will snap back in no time. You, on the other hand, I'm not so sure about. I don't think you can go on like this."

Chloe agreed. She wasn't happy, but she didn't even know how to begin to make a change. "What am

I supposed to do now?"

They both slid out from under the truck and sat up. "I don't know," he said. "I think we should both consider how to find a place somewhere in the middle. When I figure it out, I'll tell you. You do the same for me." He slid back under the truck and Chloe stood up.

"Thanks. I'm going to get back to Betsy," she said.

"Yup," he said, clanking away beneath the truck again.

When Chloe returned, Betsy had moved to a nearly upright position, but was otherwise still a wreck. "So, what did Arthur say?" She wiped her eyes with a tissue and blew her nose. A blizzard of crumpled tissues had formed next to the couch.

Chloe told her everything, starting with Arthur's denial of his brother's accusations against him, and ending with his refusal to explain why George would skip town so unexpectedly.

"That's it? He won't tell us why George left?" Betsy asked.

"He says that he can't say."

"See? It's because he's jealous or George and embarrassed of us."

"Does it seem like George would leave because of that though? He's really confident. I can't picture him being so beaten down by his twin's opinion of him that he would slink out of town."

Betsy tipped back over and pulled the blankets over her head. "I know. You're right. It doesn't make sense. But that means he's lying. Why does this always happen to me?" Betsy peeked back out and Chloe sat down next to her again. "Sorry about your shop."

"Honestly, not to minimize anything you're going through, but I'm relieved not to have to worry about it anymore."

"Really? George said you were so excited about it."

"I was conflicted, more than I was willing to admit even to myself. I never was able share the news with anyone. I think there was a big part of me that wasn't comfortable with the way things had gone surrounding the library. That wouldn't have changed no matter who the developer was. The fact that George disappeared without warning leads me to think that he's probably not a reliable business partner to say the least."

"It's going to drive me crazy not to know what happened. I thought he really liked me too."

"Unless he's a really good actor, I think he did." Chloe wasn't just saying that to make her sister feel better. She saw how George looked at her. It wasn't his usual act of laying on the charm.

"What about you and Arthur?"

"What about us?"

"Are you going to be able to move past this?"

"I don't see how we can."

"But he seems like…"

"Such a nice guy, I know." Didn't they all? She was back in familiar territory. There was something weird going on and she knew it. She'd ignored the warning signs too many times before, always having been able to find an excuse: he made her laugh, he had a flirtatious personality, he had a good reason not to tell her the truth. She couldn't keep doing the same stuff and then acting surprised when it didn't work out.

Betsy plopped her head on Chloe's shoulder. They sat side by side and watched out the window as it started to drizzle.

Chapter Twenty-One

In Which a Trip is Cut Short

The following weekend, Chloe, Wes, and Bea gathered around a table at a Thai restaurant in Madison. Chloe hadn't wanted to go. She was still conflicted about the demise of her relationship with Arthur and feeling guilty about leaving Betsy behind. Her little sister insisted that she go, though. She even volunteered to take Marshmallow for the night so Chloe wouldn't have to board her anywhere.

Once she arrived though, Chloe was happy to be getting out of town for a while. If nothing else, it would give her some literal and figurative distance from everything that had been going on. She missed Arthur and was tempted to call him, but she wasn't sure if that would mean that she was falling into her old patterns or learning to trust.

On top of that, the police still hadn't found Steve. The entire town was on the lookout, but so far there was no sign of him anywhere.

For now though, they were waiting for Wes's best friend Hugh and Hugh's boyfriend Scott to meet them there. They had been waiting for at least twenty minutes and Chloe was getting hungry.

Wes's phone beeped and he picked it up. "It's from Scott. He says they're not going to make it because..." he squinted at his phone through his glasses and read the text, "Hugh discovered a popup beer garden in Tenney Park and doesn't want to leave."

"At night? In the middle of November?" Chloe asked.

Wes shrugged. "I guess so."

"Do they want us to meet them there?" Bea asked.

"He doesn't say. I'm afraid if we head over there now, they'll be gone by the time we get there. We should probably order something and eat here. We can catch up with them later."

Chloe marveled at how laid-back Wes was about all of this. "Doesn't it ever bother you when Hugh flakes out? He does this a lot."

"Sometimes, maybe," said Wes. "But we've been friends for a long time, and he comes through when I really need him. Besides, he puts up with my quirks, and I assure you I have many."

"I can vouch for that," said Bea, squeezing his wrist. The waiter arrived and took their orders.

"So, how did the conference go?" Wes asked when the waiter left.

It was just the cue Chloe had been waiting for. "I have to tell you guys about something that happened today," she said. "I've been afraid to say anything because it seems too good to be true. It'll probably fall apart at the slightest examination but..."

"What is it?" Bea asked.

"So there I was, just minding my own business at the Great Lakes Agriculture Trade Show in beautiful Madison, Wisconsin..."

"Chloe. Stop," said Bea.

"Oh, come on. I never have news."

"Fine, go ahead."

"Ok, where was I? Oh yeah. There I was, at the trade thingy. I was demonstrating my pruning shears to an up-and-coming orchardist from La Crosse when, out of the corner of my eye, I saw someone standing at the other side of the table. She was gazing at me like I was the one she had been looking for all her life..."

"Let me guess," said Bea. "Little did you know..."

"Yes! Little did I know, she had something to tell me..."

"...that would change everything forever."

"How do you do it?" Chloe asked. "She really did tell me something that would change everything." She couldn't resist getting to the point. As much as she enjoyed telling her story, this one was too exciting. "She owns an engineering firm called Superior Valley Engineering. They design building materials and supplies for farms. Apparently I caught their attention at the show last year, and she was interested in partnering with me to expand my distribution."

"You're kidding," said Bea. "That's fantastic. I just knew it. I knew something like this was bound to happen for you sooner or later. So what's the next step?"

"I don't know. That's the thing. She wants to have a teleconference next week. I was really excited at first, but the more I think about it, the less certain I am that it's a good idea."

"Why? What did she say?"

"Not a lot. Just that they would be interested in investing in my business, assisting me with design and marketing and things like that."

"What part was concerning? Did she want to buy you out completely?"

"No. She said I would keep majority control."

"It sounds interesting at least," Wes chimed in.

Chloe nodded and took a long drink of water. "I'll be right back," she said. She walked to the bathroom. She had been so anxious to share her news, but when she started talking about it out loud, she wished she hadn't. It would've been better not to have said anything, so when it didn't work out she wouldn't have to share her disappointment with anyone else.

When she got back to the table, Wes and Bea were discussing their plans for the rest of the night. They didn't bring up Chloe's business opportunity again. They must've been able to tell that it was making her anxious. They were really perceptive and thoughtful that way. During dinner, Bea looked pensive a few times, but she never mentioned it.

They were walking to Bea's car after dinner when Chloe's phone rang. "It's Betsy. I better take this. You two can go ahead."

Betsy sounded frantic on the other line. "I am so sorry."

"What happened?"

"I was walking Marshmallow on the sidewalk when she saw a squirrel. She pulled the leash out of my hands and ran into the woods. I can't find her anywhere." It was difficult to hear her over the wind on both their ends.

"Ok. It's ok. She's done this before."

"She has? Where did she go?"

"The last time she got away, I looked for her all over the neighborhood and found her in my backyard within the hour. She was gnawing on an old tennis ball."

"I'm on the sidewalk between our houses right now."

"If she's not in my backyard, there's probably a ball hiding in the grass back there. Take it with you so you can use it to lure her in. Do you want to get off the phone and call me back in a bit?"

"Yes. I'll call you back soon, or whenever I find her," Betsy said.

"She can't have gone far. Don't worry." They hung up and Chloe trotted the rest of the way to Bea's car. She was a little more concerned than she had let on. Marshmallow had never run away at night before, and she was incredibly difficult to catch when she wanted to be.

Bea must have picked up on her nerves because she asked what was wrong the moment Chloe got into the car. "Marshmallow slipped away from Betsy when she was taking her for a walk," Chloe said. "She's looking for her right now. I'm not too worried yet, but I hope I hear back from her soon."

Bea nodded. "What do you want to do? Do you think we should drive back?"

"Let's wait a little bit and see. I'd hate to leave only to have Betsy call back in a half hour and tell me that she's found her."

Betsy didn't call, but she did send texts saying that there was still no sign of the dog anywhere. She was going to get in her car next and drive around town to see if she might have gone further afield.

"Would you guys be really disappointed if we went back tonight? We haven't even gotten to see Hugh and Scott yet." Chloe asked. They had almost made it to their hotel. It was maddening to be sitting there doing nothing while her dog was lost somewhere.

"Not at all," said Wes. "They'll understand. And besides, we would've just slept here and left early."

"I'm more than happy to go, too. I need to be getting back in the morning." Bea agreed.

"Thank you so much," said Chloe. Bea turned around and started heading north, back towards home.

Betsy called again about an hour into their drive. "There's no sign of her. I've asked some neighbors too and no one has seen her."

"I'm on my way back," said Chloe. "We'll find her together."

"I am so sorry. I ruined your trip and lost your dog."

"It's alright. It's going to be fine. I'll call you when I'm almost home." The occupants of the car didn't talk much for the rest of the drive. Chloe looked out the window and watched the dark fields and farms zip by. She wanted to be there already; the three hour drive felt like it took twice that long.

When they finally arrived, her friends dropped Chloe off at home and set out to drive around the county roads in search of Marshmallow. She called Betsy and they both agreed on their own separate areas to search.

Chloe parked at the head of the trail that went through the woods where her dog was last seen. She pulled a flashlight out from her glove box and got out of the truck. The trail, which usually looked so inviting during the day, appeared ominous in the pitch black of night. Clouds covered the sky, blotting out the light of the moon. Chloe rubbed her mittened hands together then grabbed her flashlight and scanned it across the trees before starting down the path.

"Marshmallow!" she called, kissing and whistling for her. She listened for the clank of tags or the click of nails on cement, but the only sounds came from the creaking trees. Acorns crunched under her feet again. She moved onto the grass to muffle their crackling sound and continued on her way.

A truck rolled by with its lights on. She could barely see it through the trees. Maybe she should call some more people for help. But no, it was too late now. Everyone she knew would be in bed.

As she got farther down the path, she thought she heard something crunching through the woods. "Hello? Marshmallow, come here girl." It didn't sound like her dog, though. Marshmallow ran through the woods with reckless abandon, sounding more like a wrecking ball than a person stepping carefully through the leaves. The sound came closer. She turned, shining her light into the dark forest. A pair of eyes looked back at her. She shrieked, dropping her flashlight on the path. It cracked open and the batteries fell out, extinguishing the light.

She fumbled to pick it up, groping around on the ground on her hands and knees. She picked up the pieces and dropped them several times before she was able to get them all together and reassemble them. She couldn't decide if she should stay there or run away, but her body made the choice for her. She was rooted to the spot. "Hello?" she called again.

No one answered and she scanned under the trees again. The beam of her flashlight finally caught the forms of two raccoons, scampering away across the fallen leaves. She turned around. A man stood in the middle of the path, blocking her way. She shone the light in his face and yelled.

"Chloe! It's ok. It's me," he said. "It's Wes."

"Wes?"

"Yeah. I'm sorry I scared you. Bea and I saw your truck parked over here and wanted to help you look."

"I'm sorry. I'm a little on edge."

"I get it. It's been a weird time, to say the least. I take it you haven't had any luck."

"No. Nothing so far."

Bea came running up the path. "What's doing on? I thought I heard yelling."

"It was just me," Chloe said. "Sorry about that. There were raccoons in the woods that startled me and then I was surprised by Wes."

"Oh good. I thought something was wrong. No sign of Marshmallow?" Bea asked.

"No. No sign of her," she said. "I'm going to look a while longer but you two should go home. It's getting late."

"I think I speak for both of us when I say that we want to keep looking too," said Wes.

"For sure. The sooner we find her the better," Bea agreed.

They walked to the end of the path, continuing to call, but were met with nothing but quiet from then on out. The night became so silent once the crickets, cicadas, and frogs stopped coming out to sing to each other. It wasn't something Chloe noticed later, in the middle of winter, but right now it struck her as ominous, and she found that she would have been comforted to know that there were millions of living things out there, keeping Marshmallow company. She was all alone, somewhere in the middle of that stillness and pitch. They turned around and headed back to their cars to continue the search.

They all spent another two hours looking, checking in with one another and then carrying on, but there was no sign of the wily dog. Finally, when she felt like she was going to fall asleep at the wheel, Chloe called off the search. She numbly drove home, climbed the stairs, and curled up in bed with her clothes still on. She didn't remember falling asleep.

Chapter Twenty-Two

In Which Chloe Continues the Search and Finds More Than She Bargained For

When Chloe awoke, it was still dark. Shooting out of bed, she raced down the stairs. She looked out the patio door into the backyard and flipped on the light. There was no one there. She walked outside, calling quietly so as not to disturb the neighbors. After she had stood there for a while listening, her breath curling into frosty plumes, she wandered back into the house. She grabbed her keys and jumped into her truck. She backed out of her driveway and drove down the road, not sure where she was headed.

She drove down Main Street. Everything was quiet and still. The streetlights still shone, illuminating the shop fronts and sidewalk. Where could Marshmallow have gone? Chloe pulled over on the side of the road and closed her eyes, trying to picture where her dog was likely to go after running into the woods. Maybe she should head back over to her neighborhood.

She opened her eyes with a start. Someone was tapping on her window. It was Betsy. "Hey, let me in, it's freezing out here."

Chloe unlocked the truck door and Betsy climbed in, her nose pink and frozen looking. "What are you doing out here? It's five in the morning," said Chloe.

"I'm looking for Marshmallow, same as you."

"Oh. Of course you are." Chloe tried to hide her surprise. It meant a great deal to her that her sister was out searching too. The fact that it was so early gave her efforts extra significance. Saying that Betsy was not a morning person was putting it mildly.

"Any sign of her?" Chloe asked.

"Not yet. You?"

"No. Nothing. I was just thinking about where to go next."

"Mom and Dad are out looking too."

"They are?"

"Yeah. I texted Mom this morning and it woke her up. You know how she always keeps her ringer on in case we need her."

"She does?"

"Yeah. She insisted on coming out to help."

"That's really nice of them. I feel a lot better with four of us out here looking for her."

"Me too," said Betsy, climbing out of the truck. She leaned in before closing the door. "I'm so sorry that I lost her."

"You need to stop apologizing. I really appreciate that you're out here helping."

"Well I'm determined to find her. Give me a call if you have any leads and I'll do the same." Chloe decided to drive through her neighborhood one more time. She could just picture driving up to her house to see the silly Labrador bounding out of the backyard with a tennis ball in her mouth.

When she got back home, though, the yard was still deserted. She called a little longer this time, before getting back into her truck. She smacked the steering wheel in frustration. How could a dog that big manage to just disappear? She couldn't. Maybe later, when people were awake, someone would spot her and call.

Chloe drove towards the wooded path again when her phone rang. Maybe someone had found her already. It was Arthur. Why would he be calling so early? Unless...

"Hello?" she said.

"Hey. A friend of yours showed up over here. Are you looking for her?"

"Yes! I'm out right now. Is she with you?"

"She was harassing my chickens when I went out to milk the cows this morning."

Chloe was beside herself with joy. "Thank you. I'll be right over to get her. I've been so worried."

"She's perfectly fine, and will be thrilled to see you. I think she likes it around here. I found some of Daisy's old toys for her to play with."

"Tell her I miss her. See you in a minute." Chloe called Betsy and told her that Marshmallow was safe and sound at Arthur's house.

"Really? Oh, I am so happy. I'll tell Mom and Dad. I can't believe she made it all the way out there."

"I know. Me either. I'm going to pick her up

right now."

"Tell her I'm mad at her and I love her."

Chloe laughed. "Will do."

"Will you do something else too?"

"Sure."

"You should talk to Arthur. He's a good one."

"I will; he has my dog."

"You know what I mean."

"Yeah, I do. I'm thinking about it."

"Well, think about it fast. It doesn't take that long to drive over there."

When they hung up, Chloe did think about it. She considered everything she had learned about him in the time that they had spent together. Could she trust him, even if he wouldn't tell her what happened between him and his brother? Or was she avoiding a difficult truth once again? She wasn't certain.

She could never be completely certain, but he seemed to have a great deal of integrity. Perhaps that integrity was what was preventing him from revealing George's reason for leaving. She and Arthur had barely started dating; she couldn't really fault him for not baring his family secrets, whatever they were.

Chloe didn't see anyone around when she pulled into his driveway. Getting out of her truck, she listened for Arthur's voice. The cows gazed at her with their big doe eyes from behind a thin electric fence. She thought she could hear something coming from the barn. She walked across the yard and peeked inside.

When she saw him, she felt a certainty that

crackled in the air between them. He carried the weight of something that felt unspeakable because it couldn't be changed, even with all of his goodness and light. There was no use in bandying it about. There was only accepting it and trying to let it go.

Arthur was petting Marshmallow, whose tongue hung out while she gazed at him adoringly. Marshmallow hadn't noticed her yet, but she thought that Arthur had looked her way before turning his attention back to her dog.

"I need to get something off my chest, Marshmallow, and I've heard you're a good listener," he said. Chloe leaned against the door frame, listening in. "I've tried talking to my tractor about this, but he's always interrupting me. He's very self-centered. I've given up on having that kind of a relationship with him. Anyway, you're lucky. You get to be with Chloe all the time, whereas I haven't seen her all week. We haven't even spoken. I miss her. You're familiar with all of her charms. What's your favorite thing about her?"

He waited and Marshmallow leaned into him for more scratches. "Yeah. I like that too. My favorite thing is the way that she stands up for what she believes in, even when it gets her into trouble. She looks out for her friends and family. She even saved Lindsay's barn. Did you know that?" Marshmallow didn't. "She doesn't always mean to be, but she's really funny. In fact, she's especially funny when she doesn't mean to be. She's willing to try new things, even if it means getting stuck in a puddle and having to sit next to a muddy guy in a tree stand."

Chloe cleared her throat. Marshmallow turned to look at her and bounded over, pressing her dirty paws onto Chloe's chest. "Where did you go, you rascal?" she said. "I was so worried about you." Unconcerned about the commotion that she had caused, the dog flopped down and chewed on a knotted rope.

"Oh, I didn't see you there. How embarrassing for me," said Arthur.

"Yes, I really sneaked up on you," she said. "It's ok though. I won't judge. I wanted to have a discussion with Marshmallow about something really similar."

Arthur joined her in the entrance. "Were you going to tell her that my tractor interrupts you all the time too?"

"I was, actually. He's very rude." She suddenly felt self-conscious. She realized that, in the rush to get out the door this morning, she hadn't brushed her teeth or changed out of the clothes that she had been wearing since yesterday. She tucked her hair behind her ears. "You know that's not what I was going to tell her." She reached out to take his hand. "What I was really going to tell her is that I miss you too. And I wanted to tell her my favorite things about you. I'm crazy about how your arms look in your t-shirt. They look so good that I was mad at you because of it the first time we met. I can't resist your handsome face or how you grin when you make a sneaky joke and you think no one else has caught onto it. And I'm sorry, but you also have a really cute butt."

"Is that all?"

"Yeah. That's all the important stuff...I'm kidding. Well, I'm not kidding really, but I also love how passionate you are about the things you care about. And I'll never forget when you followed me into a burning building and then slept on my friend's couch, even though you knew you'd have to wake up early and come back to your farm work. I love that you understood why they couldn't be together at the end of Casablanca. I even appreciate that, for whatever reason, you've decided to protect George and not tell me what happened with him. You have integrity and you're wise."

"So in other words, you like my butt," he said. She laughed. "And I understand why you doubted me."

"You do?" she asked.

"Sure. I can imagine that it looks really suspicious. George skipped town and blamed me, and I'm not willing to share details. I would find that strange too. I don't think it would be fair of me to expect you to trust me, although I wish you would."

"Oh. So you're not upset with me?" she asked.

"No. Not at all. I hope I can earn your trust, though, and I'm sad that we're not together. It hasn't been a good week."

"See, that's part of the problem, right there," said Chloe.

"What is?"

"You say these things, and it's like...you're too perfect. It's tough to believe that you're really like this. I'll never be able to live up to that kind of standard."

"I promise you, I'm not perfect. And I don't need you to be either."

"Tell me one thing about you that isn't perfect."

He thought for a minute. "I pick my nose," he said.

"No you don't."

"Sometimes I do."

"Fine. I'll take it, for now. It hasn't been a good week for me either. Can we start over?"

"I would love nothing more." He leaned in to kiss her and she held up her hand.

"And I would love nothing more than to kiss you right now, but I haven't brushed my teeth since yesterday morning." He raised his eyebrows. "I've been looking for Marshmallow."

"I have some extra toothbrushes lying around if you don't want to wait," he said.

"You're probably joking, but I'd like to take you up on that." She followed him inside and brushed her teeth in his bathroom. On a shelf above the toilet was an old family picture of Arthur with his siblings. Chloe picked it up. They sat side by side on a swing. It looked like the one that hung from his front porch. The twins were so small that their legs didn't hang down at all, but George already had his arms spread wide, smiling directly into the camera, while Arthur looked shyly over at his older sister. She put it back next to a little vase of dried flowers.

Arthur appreciated the beauty and complexity of life but had found a way to embrace its messiness as well. Maybe the two were more connected than Chloe wanted to admit. And maybe she could find a way to do the same, to let go of the illusion of being able to control any of it and enjoy whatever came next. She pulled her hair into a ponytail before walking out the door.

"Better?" Arthur asked. He looked so sweet and eager that she didn't reply. She didn't wait for him to kiss her this time either.

Chapter Twenty-Three

In Which More Pieces of the Puzzle are Revealed

Chloe said goodbye to Arthur and drove her dog home, smiling all the way. When they got inside, Marshmallow sprawled across the kitchen floor, exhausted.

"That's what you get for running all over town," said Chloe, giving her a treat. She sat down at the table, pushed her papers around to make more room, and opened up her computer.

She reached into the outer pocket of her laptop case and pulled out a business card. Written across the top, in bold letters, was Superior Valley Engineering. Before she could change her mind, she sent off an e-mail confirming that the owner of Bare Roots Tools would participate in the teleconference the following week to discuss a possible partnership.

She anticipated the wave of panic that would come crashing down on her, followed by a period of frantic activity in which she would try to work her fraying nerves smooth again. Instead, she felt at ease. This subsequent calm was strangely alarming, like a wide shot of still waters in a shark movie. The ominous music would begin, signaling that the great white was going to break through any moment.

She continued to work for a couple of hours, taking a break every now and then to play with Marshmallow. She hadn't even been missing for half a day, but Chloe was incredibly grateful to have her back, safe and sound. "How did you get all the way over to Arthur's?" she asked. "Were you planning to get us together all along?"

Tap. Tap tap tap. Someone was knocking at her door. She hadn't been expecting anyone. It was Tom, standing on her welcome mat with his hat in his hands.

"Hi there, Chloe," he said. "I heard I missed seeing you the other day at Arthur's."

"I heard the same. He said that you were helping him out with his greenhouse. I was just there this morning again, as a matter of fact. Marshmallow ran away and ended up appearing over there." Her dog tried to squeeze past Chloe's legs to say hello to Tom, but Chloe blocked her.

"She's alright," said Tom, "I've got a couple of big dogs like her myself." Chloe moved out of the way and Marshmallow broke free, greeting their visitor with a wiggle.

"Would you like to come in?" Chloe asked.

"Yes, if you're not too busy."

"Not at all, have a seat." Chloe led him to the couch. "Would you like anything to drink?"

"No thank you. I came here to talk to you about something, but I'm not sure where to begin…" Chloe sat down next to him, waiting. He twiddled his thumbs in his lap and she reflected that she had never seen him at a loss for words before. "I didn't mean to eavesdrop, but I heard enough of your conversation with Arthur the other day to figure out what had happened between you two," he said.

She nodded. "That's alright. We hit a bit of a roadblock, but I think we've gotten past it."

"That's good to hear," said Tom. "Arthur's a good man. Nevertheless, I still think it might be helpful if you understand some things a bit better going forward. I know I have a reputation for being a bit of a story-teller, but I'm not one for spreading rumors."

"I know you're not."

"In this case however, I'm going to share something with you on the understanding that it stays between us."

"Of course," she said. She was anxious to hear what he had to say, certain that it concerned the situation between Arthur and George.

"I've been close with the Watson family for a very long time. I stood up in Roy's and Sarah's wedding, as a matter of fact. I care about them, all of them, even if some of their members end up going astray from time to time."

"I didn't realize that you were close." Chloe couldn't picture that. Mostly because... well, Roy.

As if anticipating the full extent of her thoughts, Tom said, "Roy and I don't always see eye to eye, but we grew up together. We have more in common than you might guess. We both farmed all our lives. As much as I love it, farming can be a lonely and frustrating job. It's important to have friends who understand what things are like day to day."

Chloe agreed. Her friends in the Demeter Society reminded her how valuable those kinds of friendships were all the time.

"That brings me to the subject of Roy's two youngest sons, George and Arthur. George has always been the apple of Roy's eye. So much so, that he overindulged the boy, let him get away with things until he thought he was invincible."

"Unfortunately, I think that may still be the case," said Chloe. "Did you hear that he skipped town?"

"It is and I did. And that's the crux of the matter. He left town, in part, because of his dealings with me."

"With you? What do you mean?" This was unexpected.

"I think it would be better if I begin a little farther back," Tom said. "Several years ago, George got heavily into debt. I don't want to speculate too much but I suspect there was some gambling involved. Besides, he always lived beyond his means. Whatever the reason, one day it finally caught up with him. He had some success in his business, but it wasn't enough.

"Roy and Sarah helped bail him out with an infusion of cash, as much as they could anyway, but they also gave Arthur some money for a down payment on his farm. George was jealous. He claimed that it wasn't fair that Arthur was getting ahead while he was barely breaking even."

"But it was his own fault that he had fallen behind in the first place. What did he expect?" Chloe was galled at his presumption and sense of entitlement.

"I hear you. And I agree. Roy felt guilty about the whole thing, but ultimately he felt the same way and put his foot down. Enough was enough. In the meantime, Arthur moved to the farm and got engaged to a woman that he had met from out of town."

"Arthur was engaged? I had no idea."

"It didn't last long," he said. "Arthur tried to keep it secret from George, for reasons you'll soon discover, but George found out and decided to get revenge. At least, I assume that was his motivation." Chloe suspected that she knew where this was headed.

"George moved back for a while, claiming that he wanted to be closer to his aging parents and nieces and nephews. What he actually did was become close with Arthur's fiancée. A little too close, if you understand my meaning. So close, in fact, that Arthur called off their engagement before it had been formally announced."

Chloe was appalled. She felt awful for Arthur, and grateful that George had left before he and her sister had become even more involved. She was also starting to piece together something else. Last month, at Hannah's wedding, Arthur told George that he wasn't romantically interested in Chloe at all, which had proven to be untrue. Maybe he had been trying to avoid goading George into developing a sudden intense interest in her.

Tom continued. "George jilted the girl almost immediately afterwards and returned to the city. He had some more success in real estate development there and seemed to be turning things around. When I heard that he was coming back with his eye on the library property, I was skeptical, but Roy insisted that George was doing well and that he and Arthur had made amends.

"Some time passed and George came to me, asking me to invest in his project. I was hesitant, to say the least. But then Roy stopped by one evening and begged me to help out. I made the decision to invest for Roy's sake, not George's."

"Let me guess," said Chloe, "Your money is gone."

Tom nodded. "You got it. Arthur came to me the other day, saying that George had gotten into some kind of trouble. He lost my money and fled town. Arthur offered to pay me back from his own pocket, begging me not to pursue George. I don't know why Arthur insists on protecting his brother, after all he's done, but family ties can make people do strange things."

"That's very true."

"I refused to take Arthur's money, but he insisted. He suggested that I could help him out on the farm every now and then if it made me feel better about it. I told him that I still wouldn't take his money but wanted to help him out on the farm anyway. I suspected that he could use the company, and I enjoy spending time with him. Anyway, that's the whole story. I come off as a bit of a fool in the end, but there you have it."

"You're not a fool. You're a good friend," said Chloe. She felt terrible for how she had treated Arthur and more full of admiration for him than ever. "And I think you were right to tell me. This won't go beyond this couch." She wouldn't even tell Betsy. The knowledge wouldn't be of any benefit to her; it would only cause her more pain. She could remember George with a bit of fondness this way.

Was Sarah aware of any of this? Her children were her world and she would be heartbroken if she knew about George's duplicity. She had to suspect a large part of it, but a mother's love could endure far worse.

"I'm relieved to hear you say that you think I did the right thing in telling you," Tom said. "I wasn't sure. But I've always had a bit of a soft spot for Arthur and I think the two of you are an excellent match, if I do say so myself. I would be thrilled to pull you two out of the mud on that old logging road for many years to come."

"Thanks Tom. We'll know who to call."

Tom stood and donned his cap. He tipped it to her and left, leaving Chloe to ponder over everything that she had learned.

Chapter Twenty-Four

In Which There's Something Special for Dessert

"Here for dinner again?" Emma asked. "I've been around long enough to know the habits of darned near everyone in this town and you, my dear, are showing all the signs of turning over a new leaf."

Chloe had to agree. She had big plans for her business and a wonderful boyfriend and she was fearlessly embracing both. Well, if she was being honest, she was mostly fearless, most of the time. She could still hear a tiny strain of shark music in the far distant background if she listened carefully, but it had become fainter by the day. "I guess you can tell a lot about people from your vantage."

"Honey, I know more about my regulars than they know about themselves."

"Funny, my mom says the exact same thing about her salon."

"I believe it. People around here are just lucky that we can keep a secret. Take you for instance. You used to come here for breakfast all alone, not saying two words to anyone. You ordered eggs, whole wheat toast, and a coffee, black. Practical, on the healthier side. You'd bolt them down and run out the door like you had hounds snipping at your heels.

"In the last few months though, I've seen you here at odd hours. Today you've put off ordering for a good fifteen minutes, which means that you're probably meeting someone. Your hair is done and I think I spot a touch of mascara." Emma peeked under the table. "Cute boots too. If I didn't know any better, I'd say a certain young farmer is going to walk in that door any minute."

"You have an impressive eye for detail."

"I'm not really that clever. Betsy told me all about you and Arthur."

"I suspected as much."

"Nice catch, by the way. He's not in here much, but when he is, he's dependable: broasted chicken and a glass of milk for lunch."

"I think you may have a future as a private detective," said Chloe.

"Please don't even suggest another job for me. I'm an old woman. This is plenty." She lowered her voice. "Speaking of detectives, did they ever find Steve?"

"They didn't. If it was up to me they'd be scouring the countryside and getting the FBI involved, but apparently at this point he's just a person of interest. They're on the lookout though."

"I, for one, never liked him. He looked shifty, like he was up to something. He always refused ice cream on his pie. Tell me, what should a lady expect from a person like that?"

Everyone around town had gone from saying that he had seemed so normal to insisting that they had known all along that he was a low-down dirty scoundrel. Worryingly for her, Chloe hadn't sensed trouble brewing at all. His bizarre behavior since he left still didn't seem real to her. She wanted to find him and ask, "How did it come to this? Were you heading down a path that led to destruction from the start, or did it creep up on you, little by little, until one night you found yourself doing things that would've repulsed you years before?"

Emma scooted away. "I'll come back when your dining companion has joined you. I think this might be him now."

Sure enough, Arthur walked in and slid into the booth across from Chloe. He pulled off his hat and smoothed out his hair. The café was busy, it was Saturday evening, and Chloe noticed more than a few people trying not to look like they were peeking at Namur's latest couple. Part of her was tempted to suggest that they go back to her house for pizza instead, but if they were going to go public, this was the place to do it.

"Any luck hunting today?" she asked.

"I didn't see anything. My dad did, but he missed. I think you may need to come out with me again. You're my good luck charm."

"I thought I jinxed you into getting stuck in the mud?"

"You did. But it's a price I'm willing to pay."

"Alright. I'll come out with you tomorrow...

"Great."

"...on one condition."

"What's that?"

"Promise me that one day you won't burn down my garage while I'm sleeping."

"This again? You know I can't promise that. I don't know where this relationship is going to take us. It could end up in some very dark places. You don't know me very well. I'm an extremely devious person."

"Clearly. Did you switch out the turtle on your porch for a turkey yet?"

"I really did do that. How did you know?" He came around to her side of the booth and took both of her hands in his. "I hate to break it to you, but my only intention is to make you happy."

"That sounds alright I guess," she said, leaning into him and smiling. He was too cute.

"Does that mean that you'll come with me tomorrow?"

"Of course. I can't wait."

Emma cleared her throat. "Are you two ready to order or do you need more time to look at the menu?" She smiled as she took their orders.

When they had finished eating, Arthur asked Chloe if she wanted to come over to his house for dessert. She jumped at the chance. More food and an extension on their evening together? Sign her up. Besides, she was anxious to see more of his tidy little farmhouse.

When they got there, Chloe parked behind him

and they went in the side door, the one that led into the kitchen. In the middle of the room, next to his usual dining table, was another table, about half-sized. Its top was riddled with holes. Its legs supported a second surface down below with a matching holey pattern.

Arthur beamed at her, "Tada," he said.

"What is it?" she asked.

"Guess."

"Is it something for a game?"

"Nope."

"Is this evidence of that devious nature that you've warned me about?"

He laughed. "Nope. Getting colder."

"Is it some kind of farming thing?"

"You're getting closer. I'll give you a clue: you'll find it really useful." He went into the living room and came out with a shovel. He stuck it through one of the top holes and then guided it into the hole directly underneath. The shovel stood up perfectly straight.

It was a tool rack. Chloe wanted to hug it. It was ingenious. She could use it to store her shovels and pitchforks in the garage or bring it with her to display them at shows or...It was incredible. He was incredible. "You made this for me?"

He nodded. "I was going to wait for Christmas to give it to you, but I got too excited about it once it came together."

"Thank you. It's perfect. I love it."

"I hoped you would. A lot of research went into

this. You'd be shocked at the number of plans I found online."

"How long have you been working on it?"

"At least a month."

"Wow. I must have made quite an impression. We barely knew each other and you were already planning a construction project for me."

"Hey, if it didn't work out with us, I'd still have an awesome tool rack."

"It did though…work, I mean."

"It sure did," he said. "There's really dessert too, in case you were worried."

"I certainly hadn't forgotten about that."

He pulled a pan out of the fridge and revealed a whipped cream covered confection. "It's pumpkin torte."

He was officially her hero. Cut the shark music, cue the symphony.

Chapter Twenty-Five

In Which There are Reasons to be Thankful
(Big Ones and Tiny Ones)

"Are you sure you're ready for this?" Chloe asked. She and Arthur stood on her parents' front porch. They had gone hunting in the morning and then went home and changed for the occasion. He wore a plaid button down with a collar that was a bit askew. Chloe folded it over in the back and he kissed her forehead.

She still couldn't believe that he was here. Would she ever get over feeling giddy around him? She suspected that she may not, and that was just fine with her. It brought to mind a hike she took up and down the Grand Canyon. There was a precipice on one side, but she knew that if she kept focusing on her destination she would reach the top with its incredible view. As a matter of fact, the view was looking fine from her current perspective as well.

Arthur took one of the pies out of her hand and cracked open the door. "For the last time, it's going to be great. Experiencing someone else's Thanksgiving drama will make me feel better about my own family's antics, which you'll get to experience up close and personal this evening. We'll laugh about this tomorrow." He waved her into the house and followed behind. She hoped that he was right.

The moment they stepped through the door, her mom came running. She hugged them both and took the pie tins out of their arms. Turning to Arthur and said, "You're the man of the hour, you know. We're so happy you're here. Chloe has never brought a man to a family event. Not ever. When she told me she was bringing you, I almost tipped right over in shock."

"Mom!" Chloe objected.

"What? I just want him to know that it's a rare feat to win the heart of my middle girl."

"I do know, and I'm honored," said Arthur. He put his arm around Chloe's shoulder and pulled her in close. She didn't want her mom to see her blushing, but she couldn't help it.

"Come on in," said their hostess. "Your sisters just got here." Betsy and Hannah were at the stove, arguing over how long to simmer the cranberry sauce.

"You're both wrong," Chloe said. They were about to launch into an argument with her when they realized that she was just egging them on.

"You always do that," said Betsy.

"You should stop making it so easy," Chloe replied.

"Why don't you go into the den with the guys, Arthur?" their mom asked. "I feel a little guilty leaving Alfonse alone with his new father-in-law. I can't imagine what they're talking about in there."

"I'd be happy to go liven things up," he said. He was joking but no one else caught on. He wasn't much of a conversationalist and he knew it. What do you get when you cross a mechanic, a farmer, and a...what did Alfonse do? It was something with computers. Chloe needed to make more of an effort to get to know her older sister's new husband.

"So...you and Arthur are getting pretty serious, huh?" Betsy said. "I knew it. You two are adorable."

Hannah shook a wooden spoon at Betsy, accidentally spattering her with a spot of cranberry sauce. "Leave her alone. This is exactly what you guys did with me last year when I brought Alfonse back."

"And look where you ended up," Betsy replied, eyeing up Hannah's ring. It was quite stunning.

"Speaking of which," Hannah said. "I have to tell you guys something." The kitchen went silent. They all looked at her, waiting. "I think you can guess what I'm going to say."

"No way!" Chloe cried. "Are you pregnant?"

"I am. I just found out three days ago." They all ran to her and wrapped their arms around her.

Their mom was first to speak. "I'm going to be a grandma. I can't believe it. You girls have no idea how long I've been waiting for this." She'd been talking about it at every family event for the past seven years at least. "I knew it. I knew this would happen the second you got married. The women in my family are very fertile. Warn Arthur, Chloe. Tell him that you come from a very fertile line. He could so much as look at you and, bam, you're pregnant."

"Wow," Chloe said. "I'm so happy that we got this all in the open while he's in the den. Is there anything you want to say on this topic? Because now would be an ideal time to get it out."

Her mom thought for a moment. "That's it for now." That was ominous, but there was big news to celebrate. Chloe would save her anxiety for the dinner table.

"Congratulations," said Betsy. "How do you feel?"

"A little tired. Overwhelmed. I think I'm a little bit queasy," their mom replied.

"I meant Hannah."

"Oh yes, of course you did."

Hannah laughed. "I'm all of those things too, Mom. I know it's pretty early to be feeling much of anything, but I was exhausted last week and I wondered why. I took a pregnancy test and there was my answer. We're only telling immediate family right now, but you can tell Arthur too, Chloe."

"He's basically family now," said Betsy.

"You guys know that we've just started dating, right?"

"Details," Betsy and her mom said at the same time. They looked at each other in shock and high-fived.

"Are you already thinking about names?" Chloe asked, bringing the attention back to Hannah.

"I wanted Fitzwilliam if it's a boy, after Mr. Darcy from Pride and Prejudice. Or Elizabeth if it's a girl..."

"After your favorite sister Betsy," said Betsy.

"Right. After my favorite sister Betsy. But Alfonse isn't so sure about going the literary route. Apparently he's named after a picture book character, and he's never been crazy about his name."

"Al Capone's full name was Alfonse," said Chloe.

"Really? I'm not sure if that would make him feel better or worse about it."

"Well, no matter what you name your baby," their mom said, "he or she is going to be very lucky to have parents like you. That baby is loved so much already." She patted Hannah's stomach and hugged her again. Their mother was a mysterious woman. She alternated between being thoughtful and cringeworthy and there was no way of telling which you were going to get at any given moment. "Would you like to tell your dad at dinner?"

Hannah considered. "I'll tell him when we're taking turns saying what we're grateful for."

Hannah went back to stirring the cranberry sauce while Betsy tried to get it off the heat and Chloe took the turkey out of the oven. Most of the dishes were already set out on the kitchen island. "Does anyone want to tell the menfolk that lunch is served?" her mom asked as she set out a wheel of brie and some crackers. Her mom was really traditional. Chloe knew that, if it was up to Arthur, he would be in here helping them prepare the food. He likely had his own strong opinions on how long to cook the cranberry sauce.

Chloe volunteered to get them and tiptoed to

the den, hoping to overhear some of the fascinating conversation going on there. "Get out of here," her dad said. Uh oh. "You have a Model A Row-Crop John Deere? What year?"

"It's a 1945. It was my great-grandpa's. I've driven it in the 4th of July parade a couple of times. I always have to work on it for about a month beforehand, but that forces me to keep it up. You should come out and see it sometime."

Chloe opened the door. Her dad was getting up off his recliner. "Let's go right now."

"Lunch is served guys," she said.

Alfonse looked up at her like she was rescuing him from the top of a roof during a hurricane, but he played it cool. "Lunch is ready? Great. It smells delicious." He and her dad passed by her, but she caught Arthur as he went past.

"Way to win over my dad," she said. "You know he's going to be sneaking over to your barn all the time now so he can tinker with that tractor."

"Hey, I wouldn't mind. I could use the help. That thing is touchy. I grew up working on it, and it still presents me with a couple of puzzlers ever year."

"You didn't tell me that you had an antique tractor, by the way."

"I'm full of surprises, remember?"

"I do remember," she said, taking his hand.

"What are you two doing over there?" Betsy asked, walking down the hallway. "I'm coming to get you, so break it up." When she got there, she asked Chloe if they could talk privately. "It's nothing personal, Arthur, just some sister stuff."

"I understand. I have two sisters myself. I'll meet you two in the kitchen."

"What's up?" Chloe asked. Betsy turned serious.

"I think I might be pregnant too," she whispered. "I was supposed to get my period four days ago, and I haven't. It's never late."

"So you're not sure."

"No. I'm afraid to find out. What will I do?" They panic in her eyes matched the flutter in Chloe's chest.

"If you are, I mean to say...Is it George's?"

Betsy nodded.

"Ok. Let's take this one step at a time. Everything's going to be fine."

"You don't know that. We don't even know where he went."

"Girls?" their mom called.

"Coming," said Betsy. "I know it'll be alright, I'm just freaking out a little."

"I don't blame you, but you have all of us. You're not alone."

Betsy took a deep breath and plastered a smile on her face. The two sisters joined the rest of the family in the kitchen. When everyone was gathered around the table, their dad said grace. As was their tradition, they all shared what they were most thankful for that year. Betsy was thankful for lessons learned, even though they were acquired the hard way. *They may end up being acquired the really hard way,*

Chloe thought.

Alfonse was thankful for his new bride. Chloe's mom was thankful that her prayers had finally been answered, and Chloe was silently thankful that her dad didn't ask what she meant before Hannah had a chance to share her big news. Chloe's dad was thankful for his family and his recent discovery of a new tractor in the neighborhood.

"Get ready," Chloe whispered to Arthur. "You're about to become his second friend." Arthur grinned, clearly looking forward to it.

When it was Arthur's turn he said, "This is going to sound kind of strange, but I'm thankful that Chloe's truck broke down."

Chloe gasped. "Hear me out," he said. "Two months ago, I thought that my life was complete. And then one morning this beautiful woman showed up in front of my house, yelling on the side of the road and taking a break to talk to her truck."

"Who was it?" Betsy asked. Chloe glared. "I'm kidding! It was obviously you. Who else talks to their truck?"

"Yes, it was Chloe," Arthur said. "She seemed funny and caring and when I got to know her better, I realized that I was lucky enough to be right. She was. So that's why I'm thankful that your truck broke down, Chloe, because now I get to spend this day with you and your lovely family."

"Oh my word," her mom said. "Where have you been all our lives?"

That was the most Chloe had ever heard Arthur

speak in front of a crowd. She turned to him, blushing again. "I'm thankful that Old Blue broke down too, but don't tell her that." Everyone laughed. "It was one of many opportunities disguised as mishaps that helped me to see how lucky I am to be part of this loopy family. Hannah, you didn't go yet. What are you thankful for?"

Hannah and Alfonse looked at each other before Hannah turned to her dad. "I'm thankful that there's going to be a new member of the family. I'm pregnant."

Her mom cheered, so beside herself that it was like she hadn't already heard the news a half hour previously. Her dad, however, did something unexpected. He stood up and walked around the table. He hugged Hannah and kissed her on the cheek. "You're going to be an amazing mother. I'm so proud of you, and I can't wait to be a grandpa."

He walked back over to his seat, squeezing his son-in-law's shoulder on the way. Right before he sat down, he looked over at Chloe and smiled.

"I think it's time to eat," he said.

Author's Note

Although the people and many of the specific places in this tale come entirely from my imagination, Namur, Wisconsin is a real town and a little known National Historic Landmark in Southern Door County. It is nestled at the base of a peninsula that separates the waters of Green Bay and Lake Michigan. In the mid-1800s, Belgian immigrant families from the French speaking region of Wallonia settled the area, and it remains one of the longest-standing immigrant enclaves in the United States. The red brick farmhouses, roadside chapels, and summer kitchens still dot the landscape, and the local delicacies are on display every year at Kermiss.

My favorite part of writing, other than getting to spend time with my funny characters, is hearing from readers. Please consider leaving a review of The Midwest Farmer's Guide to Love on Amazon. All feedback is appreciated, as it helps me grow as a writer and will help direct others to a series that they may enjoy as well. Thank you so very much.

Chloe's Homemade Apple Butter

3 lbs apples
2 T lemon juice
½ c brown sugar
2 t cinnamon
½ c Linsday's apple cider (or store-bought, in a pinch)

*Peel and slice the apples and place them in a large saucepan on the stove. Add lemon juice, brown sugar, cinnamon, and apple cider and toss to coat.
*Simmer over medium heat for about fifteen minutes, or until apples are tender. Smash with potato masher or immersion blender until smooth.
*Reduce heat to low and simmer, stirring occasionally, for about two hours, or until the sauce has reached its desired thickness. Sauce should be deep brown and glossy.

Apple Belgian Pie

These pies are different from a traditional pie in that they are smaller and are topped with a cream cheese sauce. They are also rather flat, coming out as a round disk that you can pick up with your hands. They were traditionally made in huge batches. Five seems like enough to handle for the modern chef without access to a summer kitchen.

Crust:

> 3T water, slightly warmed
> 1t sugar
> 1oz yeast
> 1/3 c heavy cream or whole milk
> 2 eggs
> 2t sugar
> ¼ t salt
> 1/3 c butter, softened
> 3c flour

Apple Filling:

> 5lbs Macintosh type apples
> ¾ c sugar
> 2t instant tapioca

Cheese Topping

2 packages cream cheese, softened
3 egg yolks
½ c sugar

First, prepare the crust. Pour water in a small bowl and add the yeast and sugar. In a saucepan, cook the cream over medium heat just until a skin starts to develop on top. Set aside to cool slightly. In a large bowl, combine the next four ingredients. Add the cream and the yeast mixture. Add one cup of flour and stir. Continue adding flour, up to three cups, just until you are able to knead it without stickiness. Dough should be soft. Cover and let sit in a warm place until doubled in size.

To prepare the apple filling, peel, core, and chop apples. Cook the on the stove, adding a little bit of cider or water if needed. Smash when softened. Stir in sugar and tapioca.

To make the cheese topping just beat everything together and viola!

Divide the dough into five parts and press it into the bottoms of five greased pie tins, making a rim around the edge to hold the filling. Pour in the apple filling and spoon the cheese mixture over the center of the filling to form a circle. Bake at 350 degrees for 25 minutes.

Acknowledgements

Growing up in Wisconsin, I often visited my Belgian-American grandmother, Bernie Moore, and her proudly Irish husband Al Moore, in Namur. They passed on the value of family, traditions, learning, and the land. I hope that my stories convey a fraction of their spirit and values.

The Midwest Farmer's Guide to Love, like the other books in the Demeter Society series, grew from a desire to share a little corner of the world that is close to my heart. The history of the Walloon Belgian immigrants of southern Door County has been lovingly preserved by members of the Belgian Heritage Foundation. Their research and interviews have been invaluable to me as I write this series.

Special thanks to Mike and Margie Schwantes for cheering me on and keeping me posted on your favorite parts. I'm also grateful to Katy Schwantes for reading and editing this book. Her kind and thoughtful feedback encouraged me to ask tough questions and build a more robust and believable world.

Thank you to Cap and Mary Wulf for your promotional and emotional support and design suggestions. I'd also like to thank family and friends who so wholeheartedly supported my fledgling efforts at writing my first novel. You encouraged me to keep going, and I've enjoyed the second journey even more than the first.

To Melanie Lee, a brave, wonderful, refreshingly real person who has shown grace and beauty in the face of adversity, thank you. I know what it means to be a sister because of you.

Finally, thank you to my amazing children and my wonderful husband, Joe Schwantes. Like Arthur, he's wise, multi-talented, handsome, and an excellent chef. I couldn't ask for a better crew. I love you guys.